THINGS LOOK DIFFERENT IN THE LIGHT

AND OTHER STORIES

MEDARDO FRAILE

THINGS LOOK DIFFERENT IN THE LIGHT

AND OTHER STORIES

Translated from the Spanish by
Margaret Jull Costa

PUSHKIN PRESS

LONDON

Pushkin Press
71–75 Shelton Street,
London WC2H 9JQ

First published by Pushkin Press in 2014

ISBN 978 1 908968 18 0

Frontispiece: *Medardo Fraile* © Mercedes Rodríguez

Esta obra ha sido publicada con una subvención del Ministerio de
Educación, Cultura y Deporte de España

This book was published with the help of a translation subsidy
from the Spanish Ministry of Education, Culture and Sport

Set in 10.5 on 13.75 Monotype Baskerville by Tetragon, London

Proudly printed and bound in Great Britain by
TJ International, Padstow, Cornwall
on Munken Premium White 90gsm

www.pushkinpress.com

CONTENTS

FOREWORD

In the story by Medardo Fraile called 'The Bookstall', a man starts to buy books from a stall where the wares are generally so weathered that they've become more object than book, like rain-soaked slabs of sod—so much so that if he gives one a "squeeze" he can actually smell "the earth and the air, the rain and the sun" in it. At the end of this story, a story about inevitable disintegration, the man is living in a state of hope and delight. What he hopes is that "one day a novel would simply crumble to dust in his hands", and what has "surprised and delighted" him most is that inside his latest purchase he has found "a small, dead toad"—quite real, quite dead—"but it seemed to him very beautiful".

This is reminiscent for a fleeting moment of the American twentieth-century poet Marianne Moore who once defined our true poets as the "literalists of the imagination", the writers most able to present to their readers "imaginary gardens with real toads in them". It's a little subconscious nudge, maybe, from Fraile, for us to bear in mind that the dividing line between the forms of short story and poem is often thin and permeable, and that one of the most exciting things that literary forms can do is cross the lines, not just between each other, but between the imagined and the real, between the book and the world, to make a specific, literary and very real kind of surprise and delight.

The stories in *Things Look Different in the Light*, resonant, distilled, seemingly direct but really shapeshifting and mysterious, have the openness and the exactness of poetry. At the same time they're salty, earthy, very human stories. They're often hilarious. They're often sad. They like to appear throwaway and everyday; some perform like perfect jokes, some act the anecdote, some are so fast as to be over as soon as they begin. But every one of them chases that place where the book and the world come together—where reality, language and fiction meld to make something more revealing about all three.

Medardo Fraile died in early 2013, aged 88. He had spent his childhood and his adolescence in Madrid, but lived in the UK since the 1960s, when he left Franco's Spain. He worked for a while at the University of Southampton before settling permanently in Scotland, taking a teaching post at the University of Strathclyde in Glasgow where he taught Spanish language and literature until he retired from his professorship in the mid-1980s to concentrate solely on his fiction. Fraile began as an experimental playwright, was a writer of academic articles, stories for children, essays about cinema (this collection of stories subtly displays his cineaste love) and along with his bestselling memoir work he was also a translator into Spanish, with his wife Janet, of Robert Louis Stevenson's unfinished 1896 novel, *Weir of Hermiston*.

But it was as a short story writer that Fraile was most acclaimed and beloved in Spain, where over the decades his stories won him honours and several major prizes. *Things Look Different in the Light* is the first anthologizing of his work to reach publication in the UK—the first substantial translation of his work to be available in English. Its opening story, 'Berta's Presence', is so much about the power of the seemingly small things in life that it could be about the short story form itself. It asks readers to shift perspective on, to understand quite differently, human presence in the world.

A small child is having a birthday party. A young man comes to the party. But then a young woman whose mere presence discomfits the young man arrives too, and the man suffers a crisis in confidence and leaves the party downcast. In short, that's all that happens. But what really happens is—everything, in a comical, bitter near-tragedy for the young man, whose heart in his chest is so full of dark and light that his chest becomes a "great lighthouse", and where a tiny child not quite one year old, with no recognizable language at all, can be revealed as a force of articulation, "an amorphous, attractive being, at once yielding and terrible, who no one had ever seen in a theatre, a cinema or a café, or even strolling down the street". It is a story where someone so small, so seemingly removed from what we recognize as the usual social commerce, proves a source of epic energy, "great things engaged in vigorous movement". It is funny, and as it draws all of a sudden to its end, suddenly terribly sad. The moodswings from moment to moment in the room, the wordlessness, the unsayables, the small talk, have bristled to life in a story all about people hopelessly unable to speak to each other.

So little is said and so much is conveyed; one of Fraile's gifts is the giving of voice and language to things and states that ostensibly have none. In his writing, the sea has its own syntax. In the story called 'Full Stop', the merest punctuation mark is proof, both at once, of terrible human frailty and ebullient existence. 'Cloti', a story of a serving girl who comes from the country to a well-off family in the city, looks like a story whose only purpose is its funny punchline—but its hefty punch, when it comes to the question (in a country where people are the same nationality, share the same history but live as if on different planets) of who has voice, who hasn't and who decides who gets to speak and how, packs a powerful and far-resonating revelation.

"Life, I think, is full of surprises," as the narrator of the story called 'Typist or Queen' puts it. These stories go out of their way to de-romanticize. This is the beginning of the story called 'A Shirt': "Fermín Ulía, although poor—and from a poor neighbourhood—had already sailed, if not the seven seas, at least two or three." It begins with the puncturing and dismissal of romantic expectations; by the end of its first paragraph it has reduced the sea to "that great cod-liver oil factory… that great factory of phosphorous". Then, in the space of only a couple of pages, Fraile springs an unfathomable surprise, so that 'A Shirt' becomes a story about the mysteries that inhabit even the work clothes we mundanely wear, and one of the most romantic and moving stories in the collection.

In Fraile's work typists are queens *and* typists at the same time, just as the two ageing old spinster sisters in one of his most playful stories, 'Child's Play', can and will—and of course can't and won't—outwit their own ageing process by hanging extra glass and lights on their old chandelier. Their sitting-room furniture has to be altered to make more room for the monstrous size of the chandelier, and the light they create bleeds through the walls into the apartment next door. The neighbours complain. The landlord shrugs. "One cannot speak ill of light." There's nothing romantic about it; the chandelier is a "great jellyfish", a "gigantic udder filled with light", and the sisters become like "two old raisins filled with light". But with the final off-switch, death, both old women dead and buried go on glowing under the ground for weeks. The story pivots between gentle satire and a renewal of vision. At its heart stereotype is dismissed— "we will never be relegated to a corner", the girls decide when they're younger. Human sensitivity and strength are lit and liberated by a vital piece of comic storytelling.

Such generosity runs through Fraile's writing like electricity, or like light and flowers do, but always in the knowledge that flowers wilt and light is a matter of darkness. The people in the stories yawn, yearn, know disappointment, sense the sadness of time as it slips away, and can't do anything about it. But the stories suggest and offer a different currency, and it's typical of Fraile that Rosita, in 'The Cashier', takes the money in the café bar she works in and at the same time records, in a story about the real worth of the stories we tell about ourselves and others, "the hidden depths and ways of the regular customers" or that Luis, in 'That Novel', knows he's read a novel in which the whole of life is held, "in richer, livelier and more memorable form" than life really is, but can't remember the name of it, and the story's bathetic and funny ending is both a denial of satisfaction and a satisfaction in itself. In these stories, like in the shining 'Reparation' Fraile calls for the recognition of a different kind of accountability. A man's wife has died. In their lifetime, the man and his wife were robbed of their only substantial income. At her death the man decides to become a beggar and at its end the story calculates what is owed the man, but so exactly that the act of the story becomes a reparation in itself which resonates across all the losses, all the disappointments.

In Fraile's eyes, "the mornings were the colour of rabbits or wild boar." "The road was a strange, sleeping, endless blue vein." Miracles are an everyday matter here and the everyday so surreal that, as the narrator of 'Play it Again, Sam' suggests, why would we need cinema when the mundane is so shocking a surreality? But the real miracle in this work is the revelation of the worth, not of strangeness, but of ordinariness. "Was I the boy who was going to write *Paradise Lost* or *The Divine Comedy*?" the narrator of the bittersweet 'The Lemon Drop' says. "Something very valuable was cut short. And something perhaps far more ordinary was set in motion."

In these robust, funny, transformatory stories, Medardo Fraile, a master of the short story form, sets the ordinary alight; he graces it with an enlightening shift of vision like the kicker in a cocktail, and with an energy that's a repeating efflorescence. He reveals the dust of us as really worth something. He questions not just how we're seen and how we see, but what books are for—books like the ones on that bookstall, so wet and weather-ruined that they've stuck to the planks of the stall and have to be prised off, prised open. Inside, "those books contained the tunes he played on the harmonica, the ox carts, human time, the joy of walking the earth."

It's a real matter of delight having these stories in English at last.

ALI SMITH

BERTA'S PRESENCE

IT WAS LUPITA'S FIRST BIRTHDAY. Lupita was an amorphous, attractive being, at once yielding and terrible, whom no one had ever seen in a theatre, a cinema or a café, or even strolling down the street. But she was plotting in silence. She imagined great things engaged in vigorous movement and was convinced that she would triumph. She smelt delicious in her night attire. She smelt like a little girl about to turn one. Her parents had invited their friends over for a bite to eat. "Do come. It's Lupita's first birthday."

Jacobo rang the bell and heard familiar voices inside. When the door opened, he said loudly, "Where's Lupita? Where's that little rascal?" And the child appeared, squirming about in her mother's arms, her small body erect, excited, attentive. Lupita, in her own strange, personal language had managed to convey to her mother the idea of tying two small pink bows—like wide-set miniature horns—in her sparse, perfumed hair. It hadn't been her mother's doing at all. The suggestion had come from Lupita herself, aware of her charms and her flaws.

"So what have you got to say for yourself, then, eh? What has Señorita Lupe got to say for herself?" And Jacobo produced a little box of sweets from his pocket and showed it to her. "Baaa!" said Lupita joyfully, showing the visitor her pink uvula and waving her arms and legs about as if fearlessly leaping over each "a" she uttered. She liked Jacobo.

A bottle on the table reflected the branches of the chestnut tree outside the window. It was a warm evening, the windows open, full of the distant murmurs and melodies set in motion by the departing sun. One of those evenings on which the scented, rustling countryside suddenly enters the city, as if the countryside had left itself behind for a few hours in order to set the city-dweller humming a tune, whether at a birthday party, in a bar or at home. One of those evenings when the factory siren sounds like the moan of a large, friendly animal gone astray and where the frank, rustic kisses of the soldier and his sweetheart sound like pebbles in a stream. One of those evenings of high, long, tenuous mists, so that when the first stars come out, they will not appear too naked.

Every now and then, the doorbell rang and new friends came into the room. The engaged couple, bound together by a prickly sweetness, the wounding words recently and rapidly spoken on the landing outside not yet forgotten and transmuted instead into delicate social irony. The tall friend, in a dark, striped suit, who keeps looking at his watch only immediately to forget what it said, with the look of a man who has left some poor girl standing on a corner. The newlyweds, inured by now to everyone's jokes, strolling in as if fresh from a gentle walk, he in an immaculate shirt and she full of solicitous gestures. The desperate young woman, who can never persuade her fiancé to accompany her on visits, whose stockings always bag slightly and who has one permanently rebellious lock of hair. The sporty friend, always fresh from the shower, slightly distant and smiling and as if fearful that the great lighthouse of his chest might go out. And Berta, the outsider, the surprise, the one they had not expected to come.

They all got up again when Berta arrived. She greeted everyone—Jacobo rather coolly—and then immediately turned all her words and attention to Lupita. "Look, Lupita, I've bought you some earrings. Do you like them?" Jacobo was put out. He had been just about to speak to Lupita when Berta arrived. He had gone over to her, and Lupita was already looking at him. He was about to say: "Aren't you getting old! One year old already!" But when he heard Berta speak, his words seemed pointless and unamusing. They seemed hollow and, therefore, entirely dependent on intonation and timing. He allowed them to die on his lips, and that death was an almost insuperable obstacle to all the other things he subsequently said and thought.

Jacobo knew how difficult it was to speak to children. You had to have something of the lion-tamer about you or else limitless wit and spontaneity. Children demand a lot of those who speak to them and, unless they instantly succumb to the charm of a phrase, they regard their interlocutor circumspectly and at times harshly. They can tell when the words are sincere and when they falter in any way. They cry in terror at clumsy words or words full of twisted intentions or falsehood. And Jacobo, who had, on occasions, spoken to children quite successfully, fell silent, profoundly silent, listening to the river of efficacious words that flowed from Berta to Lupita.

That was one of Berta's qualities, knowing how to talk to children. With her subtle, imaginative intonation, Berta came out with the most wonderful things. Children stood amazed as they—intently, pleasurably—followed the thread of her voice. It was as if they had before them a fine-feathered, perfumed bird with an attractive, kaleidoscopic throat, like a grotto full of stories and legends. And Berta did not change her voice in the least; she was just herself. That voice—thought Jacobo—emerged from clean, colourful depths; it bubbled gently and was, like water, sonorous and fresh, rich and profound. More than that, Berta knew the language of children, knew which syllables to cut out and in what innocent moulds to reshape words so that they could be understood. How could one speak to them using the serious, rule-bound words used by grown-ups, words that have been through the hard school of Grammar?

"So, Berta, what are you doing here? What happened?"

And while Berta was explaining that she was spending a few days in Madrid before leaving again for Seville, where she had been sent by her company, Lupita was momentarily ignored and she remembered that, before Berta had arrived, someone else had been about to speak to her. And she turned her head, looking at everyone there, one by one, until she found him: Jacobo. Eyes wide, gaze fixed on him, she urged him to say his sentence. Jacobo noticed and grew still more inhibited. For her part, Lupita's mother, smiling sweetly, was following the direction of her little girl's eyes. Lupita even uttered the usual password: "Baaa!" But Jacobo, who, when he arrived, had managed some quite acceptable phrases, now nervously crossed his legs, stared into his glass of wine or grimly studied a painting on the wall, or else shot a fleeting glance, which he intended to appear casual, at a newspaper or some other object. Lupita felt suspicious, and her gaze grew more searching and persistent. What a strange man. It was so hard to know what he was thinking.

Jacobo refused, after much hesitation, to compete with Berta. As everyone there could see, her presence only increased his sense of his own absurdity, and so he tried hard to make a good impression. Not that he made much of an impression with his familiar long silences, his all-consuming shyness that showed itself in the form of an affected seriousness and slightly tactless, brusque remarks. He could never, with any naturalness, manage those strange verbal deviations of Berta's, those clean leaps from one word to another. "How's my little babbler, my baboon, my bouncing bean!" And it worked perfectly. Lupita—like all babies—did babble and could certainly shriek like a baboon and, at certain moments, she actually did resemble one of those neat little butter beans, all creamy and soft.

"What's so fascinating about Jacobo, sweetie? Why do you keep looking at him like that?" said Lupita's mother.

"Yes, she won't take her eyes off him," said the others.

And Jacobo gave Lupita a faint smile, accompanied by a determined, almost aggressive look that asked the usual nonsense one asks of children. But his shyness, crouching in his eyes like two dark dots, censured the words it occurred to him to say, pursued and erased them, leaving only a charmless, bitter void. There was a dense silence. Everyone was waiting for something to happen, for Jacobo to speak to Lupita. Half hidden in a corner, Berta was watching and smiling imperceptibly, curious and silent.

"It's awfully hot, don't you think?" he said.

And he said this as a warning to the others. He meant to say: "Yes, it's true, children do sometimes stare insistently at some grown-up, it's a habit they have, but we shouldn't pay them too much attention, we should simply talk about our own affairs. And it is awfully hot today. Unusual for the time of year. That's what we should be talking about."

"Baaa!" cried Lupita defiantly.

"It's usually getting cooler by now."

"Say something to the child! Can't you see she's looking at you?"

Yes, the moment had arrived. The silence and the expectation thickened. Eyes flicked from Jacobo to Lupita and back again. Slowly and terribly shyly, almost regretfully, Jacobo finally managed to say:

"Hello! How are you? Why are you looking at me like that? What's up? What do you want? What did I do?"

As if he were talking to a moneylender.

"What do you *think* she wants? Say something funny, man. Pay her some attention. That's what you want, isn't it, Lupita?"

Lupita burst into tears. She had seen the scowling black cloud advancing towards her across the room. And she hadn't wanted things to go that far. The words had left a dramatic aftertaste in the air, threatening and exciting. Lupita was crying because she had ventured innocently into unknown territory, where the somewhat stiff words exuded a certain bitterness, and where situations crystallized into impossible shapes. The daylight blinked, and the room filled with loud, laborious, rhythmical words of consolation. Lupita pouted and sobbed and wept bitterly. It lasted a long time.

The evening succumbed meekly. The clock struck the hour. Jacobo made his excuses, saying that he was expected elsewhere, then got up and left. He was walking slowly down the street, not sure where he was going. It felt slightly chilly. He was thinking about Berta, to whom he still felt attracted, about Lupita, so friendly and funny and lovely, and about his friends, his old friends. How nice it would have been to have stayed with them to the end.

WHAT'S GOING ON IN THAT
HEAD OF YOURS?

P<small>ACO EL LARGO</small> was my best friend at the time. The one I saw most often. I had another friend, too, who was a coal-man. But I never really knew what his face was like, still less what he thought. We used to chat in the coal-yard where he worked, and my impression was that he was rather fair-skinned. I must have seen him dozens of times outside of work, but I never knew it was him; and *he* never said hello either. Through such friends, however, I acquired some very picturesque acquaintances, people I don't even give the time of day to now. We had fun, even when we didn't have a penny to our names. Paco, especially, knew a lot of people and, now and then, thanks to him, we'd organize a really good shindig, sometimes even with a few Gypsy musicians laid on.

Family life and the family house—always dimly lit, with the shutters half closed—bored me rigid, and when it came to choosing between spending the evening with my family or going out on a spree with a friend, it was hardly a difficult choice to make. It was my mother, I think, who first started nagging me—when I was alone with her and my father and at mealtimes—about my friends and, even more, about my future.

As I understood it, my life was deemed to have taken a displeasing and, needless to say, suspect turn. It was summer—which we were spending at home—and I realized that they were all determined to put a stop to my propensity for idleness. My father, it seems, had never been like that—like me that is—and this, it seems, was accepted by everyone as an irrefutable argument. My father was also shorter than me, despite being older, and yet it would never have occurred to me to reproach him for his lack of height. But it *would* have occurred to them. They disapproved of any aspect of myself that did not resemble him. They wanted me to be a sort of second edition of my father.

All this happened in the year when my uncle Alberto decided that I should apply myself to my studies. Frankly, I had absolutely no desire to pick up a book, but my uncle had got it into his head that the phrenological characteristics of my frontal bone indicated a studious turn of mind. My uncle Alberto was—and still is—a young man; he had three university degrees, was keen on trout-fishing and going out on the town at night, plus he was my father's favourite brother, and all these factors weighed so heavily in his favour that they proved very hard to resist, given that everything was now focused on making an honest man of me.

One day, he called me into his office.

"My dear nephew, you are probably thinking, 'What on earth does my uncle Alberto want with me?'"

I looked at him. I didn't think him capable of setting a trap. He talked a great deal, and what impressed me— and this was doubtless done for dramatic effect—was that he stood right next to the portrait of my grandfather. He put his case to me almost casually, as if it were as simple a matter as putting stamps on a letter. My grandfather—long since dead—agreed with everything he said. I don't recall ever in my life having seen a portrait take such an active role in a perfectly ordinary conversation as that portrait of my grandfather, moving his eyes and lips and generally demonstrating his agreement in such a variety of ways. At the time, such things made a great impression on me. Nevertheless, I said what I thought, I didn't hold back. I told him that I would much prefer, for example, to do what my friend Paco el Largo had done.

"And what did your friend Paco el Largo do?" asked my uncle.

"He got a job in that new hotel on the Gran Vía. And this summer he's going to work on La Toja."

"Does he speak any languages?"

"Sort of."

"I see."

"You know, just what he learnt at school."

"And where does he work? In reception?"

"No, he's a waiter."

I proved easy enough to persuade. I was still pretty naive at the time. My uncle said the most amazing things about me and seasoned the dish with tales of fishing. He gave a nod to Socrates with one of his jokes about Pliny and fishing for trout with hemlock. He said that hemlock resembled parsley. The result was that when I left his office, I started turning the idea over in my mind.

"I could be a gentleman and not like Paco el Largo. After all, a university degree is a university degree. My uncle's quite right. Not everyone is as intelligent as me! And yet I…"

These thoughts carried me to the University. It was a curious world full of very pompous people, whom one gradually got used to. The girls weren't like that. They were ordinary and pretty and often burst into tears. Generally speaking, the girls led a life of leisure in the afternoons, quite different from ours. We gave ourselves over to scepticism, getting chilled to the bone and talking. Many of us spent the afternoons recovering from colds. Everyone hated the textbooks. As an antidote, they looked up the catalogue numbers of French novels to collect from the same pharmacy, namely, the library.

Some people were studying English and they would gaze out of the windows in the direction of the Atlantic. The big windows were splendid, providing excellent views of the Guadarrama Mountains and of El Pardo, and the mornings were the colour of rabbits or wild boar. Some students did nothing but study; others devoted themselves to art. I particularly noticed the sculptors and sculptresses. They were never splattered with clay nor did they have the hands of stonecutters. I found that odd. But then they were only beginners.

My uncle asked me how things were going and, as I was telling him, he offered me a cigarette, and I noticed that his hand was trembling. He didn't look well, and yet he wasn't ill: it was those wild nights on the town. Suddenly, he raised his eyebrows and said:

"My dear nephew, I may not be much older than you, but I'm old enough to tell you that, at your age, one must be very careful. Now is the time to study. Even if your eyes are drawn to a shapely pair of calves, forget them and apply yourself to your studies. No, don't laugh."

I, of course, was laughing from sheer lack of imagination.

"Don't laugh. I'm not saying you should become a saint, but don't fall in love."

"Uncle, please!"

"If you *are* ever foolish enough to fall in love, you'll begin by selling the book you need least and end up

selling the one you need most and spending the money
put by for your fees…"

I learnt nothing of note during that first year. I read—
off my own bat—*Don Quixote* and the Bible, more out of a
sense of pride than anything else. It's odd, but the Bible
is a book I'd really like to talk about one day. As for *Don
Quixote*, my reading left me only with a few choice quotes,
the most popular of which was what poor Dorotea said
about how the eyes of the lynx cannot rival loving or
idle eyes. I even tried to learn a bit of Greek to humour
a lanky, shabby fellow, who said to me one day:

"Study Greek! That way you will discover the tepid
dawn delights of *pornai*."

"Really?" I said.

"Yes, and Aristophanes will season your mind with a
little Attic salt."

Despite this, Greek did not agree with me.

But I haven't yet told you the funniest part. To me it
seems like the third act of all that went before.

In some classes, we always had to sit in our allotted
places. The teacher's register was like the fate that, day
after day, placed us next to the same person. The girl
who used to sit on my right was tall and had brown
hair. She wore a grey coat, buttoned right up: she was
a broom in skirts. She spent each morning freezing; she
even smiled coldly and had no talent at all for asking
questions. Sometimes she would ask something, but it

was impossible to understand what it was she wanted to know. Her name was Obdulia Ramos García, and my uncle Alberto had no reason to fear her. She studied quite hard. In that respect, she was like the other girls, who were always swapping lecture notes. I led a rather more irregular life. Sometimes I read in the library or attended classes. At others, I would go down to the bar, stroll about in the corridors or the garden. The garden was nice, but a bit cold at that time of year. The lines of rose bushes, with their greyish, woody stems, looked to me like adolescent orphans from the School for Rosoideae. They had no leaves and were just twigs adorned with a lot of reddish thorns. I couldn't believe that this bare scaffolding could represent something as exquisite as a rose. But then that was the world for you: a trick and a swindle. It turned out that the girl sitting on my right was exactly like one of those grey-brown twigs. She represented something equally exquisite, Woman, and she, too, wore a grey coat.

When the fine weather came, the university girls got out a long piece of rope, like the serpent from Paradise, and started skipping in the garden. One morning, I joined them, and my wintry thoughts thawed considerably. On the parterre, the first rose bush I saw had two huge roses on it. And Obdulia had taken off her grey covering, her grey coat, and bore not the slightest resemblance to those winter rose bushes. She was far more like that springtime bush, with its two roses in full bloom. She looked radiant, really lovely, as if she were waiting to be discovered by some film director. It really was most odd!

I finished the year and they gave me the slips bearing my exam results; like lilies they were, like daisies, to be floated down the river on a summer's afternoon. Wild horses couldn't drag me to Uncle Alberto's house now, and I haven't been back to the University. Some of the other girls used to ask Obdulia about her boyfriend. She told me they thought I was a bit of a dreamer. And yet for a year and a half, my head was filled with some very real plans. First, I wanted to be a merchant seaman, and then I thought I would drop the navy and study for three years to become a lawyer.

My uncle Alberto passed me in the street one day.

"What's going on in that head of yours?" he said.

At home, this was a common enough statement, as common as "Turn the radio on", "Don't be late" and "Close the door properly." A few days later, Obdulia asked the same question:

"What's going on in that head of yours?"

It was as if the world were sitting around watching, making me the centrepiece of some spectacle. Perhaps it's some kind of ancient custom, wanting to know what other people are thinking.

Lázaro—a friend of mine—used to pass me in the street every day, when Obdulia and I were out for a walk or looking for a café where we could sit. I saw him today and he stirred my memories.

"So, what happened to the girl?"

"Oh, it ended."

You see, my relationship with Obdulia ended six months ago, on my birthday, when my aunt Cristina gave me the pearl-grey hat.

Now that I have nothing to do, I enjoy remembering these things…

A SHIRT

FERMÍN ULÍA, although poor—and from a poor neighbourhood—had already sailed, if not the seven seas, at least two or three. He lived at the top of a steep hill, where, between the windows of the houses, the women hung the clothes out to dry on thin halyards that had long since exchanged sails for shirts and nappies. The early hours were always full of comings and goings, and dawn broke with the light of lanterns. Fermín, you see, was a fisherman. He went every day to that great cod-liver oil factory—the sea—to that great factory of phosphorus.

The sea had seen him on board a 2,500-tonner and on much smaller vessels too, in rowing boats and the like. But Fermín Ulía, that traveller of the mysterious, unfathomable depths, knew nothing of love. Love was to be found walking down a street. Love came in the form of inky hearts that covered your arms like a rash. It was a windward love, with lips of tar and a soul of sawdust. It was bounded by desire on the one side and, on the other, by a humorous phrase tattooed on his chest: "I killed her because she was mine." Love was there in the talk of fishermen rowing towards the fishing ground. A damp, sluttish love, an aperitif spiced with jokes. Fermín Ulía had never embarked on the journey of love, which, they say, is unfathomable and mysterious. He racked soul and brains for a way to set out on that voyage with one of those girls who haunt the ports looking for a bit of excitement in life. Meanwhile, chance brought him ashore at Dover, along that arm of the Atlantic that the French call La Manche—"The Sleeve". And out of that sleeve Fermín pulled a tartan shirt, a fate marvellously cut short, and a fair-haired woman.

It's true that the sailor arrived in Dover with the appropriate temperature for a young man fishing for love. Inside the boat, two empty bottles of brandy were all that remained of the salve he had applied to his longing to find love. But the presence of that girl in the port was enough to magnify the word Dover on the pink map of England. Her body and her fair hair stood out against the tar-daubed wall like a poster advertising a film. She was a genuine blonde, a blonde from the north, whose finer points were, moreover, as fine as those on the compass rose, although, of course, far fewer. Her name was Maureen, but she called herself Mari, María, like any nice young girl. When Fermín got off the boat and looked at her, he felt as if he were standing in the glare of the lights of a mail boat. He stood staring at her for a full three minutes, two of which he devoted to her nose alone. She had a turned-up nose that made her look as if she had a cold, but a very attractive cold, with no complications. They both smiled when they saw each other. There was no point in talking; after all, they would never be able to understand each other with words, only with looks. They both suddenly laughed. The sailor showed the girl the bottle of brandy he had concealed under his sou'wester jacket. He was going to swap it for something more English in a warehouse in the port. They went off together, eyes still fixed on eyes, responding to that most elementary mimicry, the smile.

They entered the so-called Modern Warehouse, which was actually very old and smelt of the customs and fashions of yesteryear. The assistants yearned for lost refinements and it would have taken only the pricking of a rose thorn for them to die. Fermín and Mari exchanged a first kiss behind a mannequin carrying an umbrella. Mari's lips were as tasty as the anchovies caught by night fishermen in fine mesh nets. They strolled through the warehouse, and she chose for him a tartan shirt in subtle shades. With a knowing wink, Fermín showed the assistant the bottle he had with him. Mari stepped in to prevent the exchange and held out a few coins instead. Fermín Ulía understood her meaning. They drank the bottle of brandy together in a small room with blue painted walls. And there he first put on that subtle shirt, which was all the colours of a cuttlefish on heat.

Dover was left behind along with the blonde girl. Fermín returned to his own community, where he went fishing every day wearing his tartan sailor's shirt. The memory of his love washed over him whenever the tide receded. In dreams, he saw Mari swimming among voracious porpoises. He woke in a panic. His memory, moored for ever alongside that girl, sent him fishing for scad and mackerel as if he were a schoolboy off to play truant. He would lean on the side of the boat, lost in thought, and it was clear that a wave—the very small-est—could carry him off at any moment.

The really odd thing, though, was what happened in the early hours of the morning when the sailor and his shirt failed to go off together to fish. The night was a softly welcoming, almost gelatinous lap, and the sea was like the sigh of a young boy. The shirt, with its newly washed greys and violets, yellows and pinks, had been hung out on a line to dry. The fisherman—along with his thoughts—was setting off to the fishing ground. At around four o'clock in the morning, with no wind to speak of, the shirt began to move. It flapped wildly about, anxious and empty, as if wanting to break free from the pegs gripping its shoulders. The flailing sleeves rose and fell, filled by the invisible lament of some terrible tragedy. They occasionally joined wrists or else stretched out wide, arms spread. And the body of the shirt, pegged by the shoulders, writhed and bowed again and again as if tormented by a mysterious breeze. Then it hung rigid, exhausted, stiff as a board, its sleeves pointing at the ground.

Fermín Ulía drowned at sea at about four o'clock that same morning.

TYPIST OR QUEEN

I HADN'T REALLY given Carmencita a thought in ages, but, this afternoon, I had a long conversation about her with Dimas—not the one from the Buying department, but the bald one. Dimas usually pops in to see us in the Social Affairs department when he's finished his tea break. He's in Materials and Construction, which is where Carmencita was for the first six months, when she first arrived. Then they moved her to the Technical Office, and now she's no longer with us.

I remember that the lovely Carmencita's arrival in Materials and Construction coincided with a film starring Marilyn Monroe: *Storm in the City*, I think it was, or was it *Rainy Afternoon* or *Love on the Sea*? Well, a person can't be expected to remember everything! Anyway, Carmencita's arrival and the release of that Marilyn Monroe film happened simultaneously. Some of the men, among them Dimas, even jokingly sang her the theme song from *Love on the Sea* or whatever it was called.

Initially, Carmencita was quite shy. It's always the same when new typists arrive: they worry about how fast they can type and that kind of thing, until they learn that they can type more slowly and no one's going to eat them. And they're always tugging at their skirt, although, of course, that's just a trick to make us notice that they're wearing a skirt. Carmencita was a sensation. We all referred to her as "the girl", because we were fed up with the other "women" and wanted to single her out. Had the girl arrived on 6 January, we'd have thought her a gift from the Three Wise Men; had she arrived on 21 March, we'd have taken her for Spring itself. Anyway, what happened was all very strange.

One day, this new typist arrived in Materials and Construction and, five minutes later, the whole place was in a frenzy, talking about her. And she wasn't even particularly striking and hardly wore any make-up. But there was something about her. Morán and Manolo immediately went and combed their hair and their respective moustaches, wore a new suit two weeks running and said: "She'll have to choose one of us." And they made a point of making frequent visits to Materials and Construction. But Carmencita didn't see them. She didn't even notice them, not at all. Then, of course, they turned against her. They started saying how she put on airs, was stuck-up, on the lookout for a Prince Charming and so on. But that wasn't true. Carmencita knew what she wanted and was waiting, and Morán and Manolo ended up falling head over heels in love with her. Dimas and I were glad she ignored them. I mean, even if you do earn nine hundred and fifty pesetas a month, good looks can only get you so far.

Anyway, we were talking about her this afternoon. Rosarito, the secretary in my department, couldn't stop laughing when she heard us, a cruel little laugh, as if she couldn't understand our purely altruistic interest in the girl. Women, as we know, are not always very nice to each other. The girl knew this, too, and she had a bit of a rough time of it with some of her female colleagues, as well as with the wife of a male colleague. When she was with the other women, they would put on a good front and pat her smooth cheeks, but when she wasn't there, they would say she was frivolous, arrogant, mad and—and this was what really irritated me—that she really wasn't anything so very special.

That wasn't true at all, and she certainly wasn't mad. Because I—and many of us men—occasionally went to the cinema with her, and we know that she wasn't the slightest bit mad. We were colleagues, in and out of the office, but nothing more. You might be in the cinema, say, and you'd get it into your head that she was the girl for you. Then she would give you a look, and you knew at once that you were being a fool, and at precisely that moment, she would say:

"Come on, don't spoil things. You're a colleague, nothing more, which is why I agreed to come to the cinema with you in the first place. Don't be silly, and keep your hands to yourself."

And because of that, some of the men said she was cold, but when you looked into her eyes, you could see there was a fire burning there, no, more than that, a bright blaze. She was a most unusual girl. She was the only typist who didn't want to marry any of us, and she could have if she'd wanted, just ask Manolo and Morán, not to mention Moro.

Bernardo Moro works in the Technical Office and his wife died four years ago. He's a good colleague and a serious fellow, but he's very vain and doesn't like to be told No. He's also a bit of a hothead and he spent about three years barely eating or sleeping, barely living. He really fell for her in a big way and had a very bad time of it.

What I liked best was when Carmencita would peer round the door and say "Hi!", then turn away without coming in, as if she'd forgotten something or had gone off to look at who knows what. She was just gorgeous then, because she had her own little world, you see, her own private world. The fact is that, during the three years she spent with us, she turned the office into an aquarium, in which we dull grey fishes prided ourselves on having among us a beautiful gold fish, who deigned to spend eight hours a day working to earn a wage, just like the rest of us. She was a lovely fish, long and golden, with succulent flesh, and if she'd been cut up on the slab, she'd have fetched a very good price, but that would have been a great shame. She dressed simply and elegantly, and, next to her, we felt like complete nonentities, because her presence made you think of cruise ships, tennis games and big cities: New York and Paris. As bald Dimas used to say:

"Some girls are real gems."

When they moved her from Materials and Construction to the Technical Office, where she worked more as a secretary than a typist, she again wrong-footed everyone. Including me. I got it wrong too. The Technical Office, if you like, is home to the bosses, and we immediately thought that Carmencita, as was only logical, would end up in the hands of Don Tomás, who is a fat, impulsive fellow, but he has money and position, and we all knew what he was like. He's a man of the world and knows how to give a girl a good time; well, a girl who suddenly finds herself being picked up from work by a car can get all kinds of ideas in her head. But with Carmencita nothing happened, and we know that Don Tomás plied her with endless offers and attentions. Some say—and we know who—that, one day, Carmencita slapped him. But we're not sure she would ever have gone that far. The truth is that the girl wasn't, as we had often thought, interested only in money, even though Don Tomás, being married, always went out of his way to avoid scandal. As I said before, women have a will of their own, and Carmencita knew what she wanted and, quite rightly, was prepared to wait patiently.

Today, Dimas spent a good hour and a half talking to me about her. We all took a bit of a break actually, and I even phoned down to Joaquín in the café to ask him to bring me up a coffee, which I never normally do. On some afternoons in the office we have a really good time. We talk and talk, and before you know it, it's half past seven. Anyway, today Dimas had met Carmencita in the street and, according to him, they stopped to chat. She sent her regards to everyone apparently, and Dimas said she was really friendly. Inevitably, we all ended up talking about Gaspar. I tried to take a cool, objective view. Life, I think, is full of surprises, and sometimes you just have to leave passion to one side. Gaspar was one of life's surprises. For a month or two, I remember, he was the centre of attention here. How he got the job we still don't know, but he would turn up late every morning and, now and then, he would shout at the boss like nobody's business. At first, we rather admired him; everyone talked about him and it was said that he'd saved the boss's life at the front in Teruel, that he'd been an officer and goodness knows what else. No one much liked him, though. He was arrogant, he seemed to have played even more golf than the Prince of Wales and he was a bit of a dandy. I tend to think he was a decent enough fellow, but, then again, he was one of those ill-disciplined people who spend more than they earn.

I have no idea what Carmencita could have seen in him, but that was it—end of story. They got married, had a big, expensive wedding—that was when Alberto and María Luísa from the Commercial Section first started going out together—and shortly afterwards, Gaspar got into some kind of "bother" at work, was given the sack, and Carmencita immediately asked to be transferred to the branch in Calle Méndez Núñez, where she still works now.

Rosarito, the secretary in our department, finally took an interest in the conversation and asked Dimas if Carmencita had had children after she married or if she was expecting. Dimas didn't know. He hadn't noticed and didn't like to ask.

I haven't seen Carmencita since she left and hadn't really given her a thought in ages. Dimas said she's not a shadow of her former self, not in the way she dresses or anything.

It occurs to me now that the time Carmencita spent with us was like the reign of a queen. We were better men then, because her presence required us to be. It's a reign much missed by all those who lived through it. It somehow raised us up and, every day, our heads were filled with dreams. What do these new boys, these youngsters, know about what happened to us in the past! They will never experience the reign of such a queen.

CHILD'S PLAY

As THE YEARS PASS, the winters seem darker and colder, the spring unsettling and fickle, and the rays of the summer sun seem wrapped in a distant, leaden cloud that drains them of energy. As the years pass, the flowers are only flowers by name. Their colours and perfumes largely fade. "Here are some flowers for you," we say one day to please our aged grandmother. She cautiously holds out her hand, for she can barely see the colours or smell their perfume, but, because we used the word "flowers", she looks at them as if we had presented her with a bunch of fresh memories and bestows on them a faint smile, slightly sad and distant. Old people notice how the world is growing gradually dimmer and, at the moment of death, what they really think is that someone has turned out the light, what little light they still received. In their long journey through illnesses and ailments, old people often find that they have developed cataracts, and their youngest relatives quite forget how bright those eyes were years ago. It is at this point—at least in the provinces—that older people get on a train and come to the city to walk through its streets and noises, wearing, over one eye, a white bandage that flattens the old ladies' coquettish coiffures of soft, shiny, white hair. They come to the city to visit a good doctor, a doctor with a fine reputation who offers hope, and they pay as they leave, retrieving bank notes from complicated interiors, from hidden pockets or thick wallets and belts wide enough to contain seeds and tools.

Flora and Martita could have defined old age as a darkening of the world, for that was something they knew all about. They lived in a city and finding a good doctor would have been easy for them, but they wanted to avoid doctors and darkness and so sought their own remedies. Flora and Martita remembered how the life of their mother, may she rest in peace, had come to a virtual halt because of her loss of sight; she couldn't read or knit or go out alone to visit a friend. Martita and Flora had to speak to their mother in an especially lively, jolly, colourful way, because then she saw things much more clearly. They continued to talk like that, with just as much verve, even though their mother had long since departed this vale of tears. Now—let's not beat about the bush—they, too, were little old ladies, Flora slightly more so, because she was the eldest.

They lived alone, lit by the beatific light of spinster-hood, which sometimes flickered and sometimes faded.

They had a few savings, shares in the state monopolies of explosives and tobacco, some government bonds and a tiny income from the bits of land and small houses they owned. They ate frugally and were skilled at working with ribbons and threads and fabrics; they were very pale-complexioned, well turned out and, in their simple ablutions, used water, soap, cologne, talcum powder and, occasionally, a little rosemary alcohol.

Their one eccentricity was their need for light, a little more each day. They needed light so that their hair would shine and their eyes sparkle as they had when they were twenty, so that they could knit jerseys and sell them to sailors or give them away to children, could read the headlines in the newspapers, scrutinize photographs of the Holy Father in magazines and still be able to pick out the bees and the ducks on cross-stitch patterns.

It was Flora's idea. One day, Martita had a final falling-out with her fiancé Nicomedes and all because, once, during their engagement, she had refused to go through a doorway, a very dark, ugly doorway, through which they had to pass, it seemed, to take coffee and biscuits with an aunt of Nicomedes', who had insisted on meeting her. Nicomedes had made her traipse all the way there for nothing; he was both irresponsible and flighty. Flora—who had long before bidden farewell to any hope of marriage—soothed her sister, saying:

"Marta, don't cry. You and I will remain for ever young. Your eyes and your hair will shine just as they do today. We will never be relegated to a corner. We will be the loveliest little old ladies in the world. When the men of today are old as well, they will think how wrong they were not to pay us more attention. You'll see, Martita."

And Martita watched Flora climb up the ladder to reach the crystal chandelier. This magnificent chandelier, with its engraved pendants and slender, upswept gilt arms, hung in the room where Flora and Martita kept their finest heirlooms, where they could see the umbilical cord of their lineage in the smallest knick-knack, each one silently evoking a memory. Flora did not do very much. She merely added another pendant, securing it to one of the arms with thin wire. Flora wanted to fill the chandelier's arms with bulbs and crystals. This was her money box, her hoard of light, for when she and her sister were old.

The crystal chandelier, whose centre resembled the segments of a fruit, found its arms transformed into swans' necks, into S's, and extended its domain as far down as the carpet and the furniture, like a great jellyfish or an upside-down Christmas tree or a gigantic udder filled with light.

In the evenings, Flora and Martita would install themselves in that room and, sitting opposite each other, very erect in their respective armchairs, they would knit away, never dropping a stitch. The knitting needles were like steel foils engaged in fierce combat, with neither side winning. "Click-click, click-click," sang that terrible, unending duel. The buckles on their shoes shone, as did the tortoiseshell combs in their hair, the grey pearl earrings set in old gold, the satin chokers slightly eclipsed by their double chins. Everything shone, even the sharp click of the needles.

Flora and Martita had an enthusiastic collaborator in their task: old Matías, who was a neighbour and an electrician, but no ordinary electrician. Matías would go to the house now and then to attach metal hooks to the chandelier so that Flora and Martita could hang more crystals from it, or else he would make new bulbs bloom forth or design and fit still more long gilt arms which, in his spare time, he would endow with their own translucent Spring.

Incredible though it may seem, they had to make some of the furniture in the room smaller. They summoned a carpenter to saw off legs, and a builder was brought in to reduce the height of the marble fireplace. The console table, dining table, chairs, armchairs, the large chest and the cuckoo clock all had to be reduced in height. So vast and intricate was the crystal chandelier that its arms touched the four walls of the room and nearly reached the floor, stopping only half a metre away. In the evening, it was a veritable forest of glinting crystals, a bag of light, a labyrinth, a hanging city. It had to be secured to the ceiling by five chains when it reached its prime, its peak, when Flora and Martita were old, too old, and sat beneath the chandelier like two transparent raisins filled with light.

But all this meant that they could see perfectly, well enough when they were ninety years old to be able to follow the flight of flies about the room and spot the stains on the dresses of visitors and even the greasy, open pores on certain ladies' faces. It was both a glory and a second youth.

One day, the next-door neighbours—truculent, unpleasant people—complained to the landlord that light was penetrating through to them from the old ladies' apartment, and that the affected room was filling up with light.

The landlord didn't know what to do. Leaving the light on in a room for two or three hours wasn't the same as leaving a tap running. It was light, it wasn't a leak. It wasn't a miracle, it was an unusual, unexpected occurrence for which there was no punishment, no fine, and the generous response would perhaps be gratitude. One cannot speak ill of light; it's rarely something people complain about, and so the neighbours' complaint remained unresolved.

Beneath the light, Flora and Martita were gradually

becoming small blurred shapes. They went through a phase of knitting with Lurex yarn, and the balls of wool, like creatures in an aquarium, would glint as they shifted proudly and languidly about on the floor with each tug on the thread. Flora and Martita would sometimes place on the table two glasses of liqueur, which they barely touched, just to see the light penetrating the colourful, intoxicating kingdom of alcohol. Their eyes expressed the very slightest movement of their hearts. That room contained their kingdom of light, their great invention, the torch that would allow them to see until the very end of the world. They wanted no shadows. The light filled everything, smoothing out even the most flagrant wrinkle. Thus they achieved what all women most desire—to be for ever young, to erase time.

When the fairy of time switched off Flora's light for good, Martita was left alone beneath the chandelier, waiting for her inner fuses to blow as well. The crystal chandelier became a great candle lit in remembrance of Flora and occasionally something else glimmered in the room: Martita's tears.

Underneath the earth, Flora still gave off light. Her body phosphoresced in the darkness like a female glow-worm in the night. This lasted for about three months, then gradually died like an ailing star, like a weary planet or like those astral bodies that collect light in order to transform it into something else.

When they buried Martita, her light lasted longer than Flora's—twenty-two days longer. And light poured forth from her—pink, yellow and green—as if, in its final moments, Martita's sleeping body had become a mesmerizing source of illusion.

THINGS LOOK DIFFERENT
IN THE LIGHT

LUCIO ARRIVED at the construction site at the entrance to the Metro. There were large drums and coils of rope on the stairs going down and piles of sand in the passageway. The air emerging from below was impregnated with a fine, moist dust, and you could hear the distant sound of hammer drills. Lucio was carrying pots of red, black and white paint, brushes large and small, a ruler and, in his back pocket, a folding yellow wooden yardstick. He continued down the passageway. He had to find Señor Ramiro.

"Ask for Señor Ramiro," the Metro company had told him.

There were lights down below, scattered randomly about. Voices and metallic noises reverberated all around, and every blow or voice echoed and re-echoed. The bulbs hanging from the roof were lost in the depths like dim party lanterns on a sticky, sultry city night.

"Excuse me, do you know where I can find Ramiro, Señor Ramiro?"

"Yeah, go to the north exit and turn left."

Lucio had no idea where the north exit was. He peered down the stairs in search of the platform. The last few steps seemed to be blocked off by a tall barrier. He went down the steps to the barrier and pushed gently. A door opened and there was the platform.

"Excuse me, do you know where I can find Ramiro, Señor Ramiro?"

"In the control booth."

The cabin on the other platform was finished and crammed with tools.

"Excuse me, is that the control booth over there?"

"Yes, you can either cross by the plank or use the ladder."

Lucio thought about it. He was used to walking across planks, but what if he stumbled? He was carrying a ruler, some brushes, pots of paint, and his overalls were, as yet, spotless. He had to remain spotless until he had spoken to Señor Ramiro. He felt nervous. It was the first time he had worked in the Metro. In the booth he could see a fat man in blue, his hands in his pockets and his gaze fixed on the platform opposite. Keeping his eyes trained on that blue figure, Lucio began walking across the plank. It wasn't secured at one end and wobbled slightly when he took his first step. Two men in wellington boots passed underneath him, talking loudly; they were carrying lamps and lifting their legs up high as they walked, as if they were wading through water, against the current. Dazzled by their lamps, he almost missed his footing, but managed, with a leap, to land safely on the platform. He went over to the booth. The man in the blue uniform was looking at him.

"Excuse me, where can I find Señor Ramiro?"

"That's me."

A pocket watch hung by its chain from a nail on the wall. Señor Ramiro started, glanced up at the watch, then, turning to face Lucio, said: "Dammit, man, what sort of time do you call this?" And he repeated it twice, so he obviously meant it. He said they'd phoned him aeons ago to say that a painter would be coming, so long ago, in fact, that he couldn't even remember when it was.

"Yes, but when you think about it," said Lucio by way of excuse, "the work doesn't really need to be done at a particular time. Here, you can work as late as you like. There's time enough to paint twice as many signs, Señor Ramiro."

"All right, all right. Pick up your brushes and get to work."

Señor Ramiro resumed his "work", standing as before with his hands in his pockets and keeping his gaze fixed straight ahead.

Uncertain what to do, Lucio glanced at the panels intended for advertisements. He didn't know where to start. He had to put: "Trains departing from this platform call at…" with a line underneath followed by the names of the stations that the trains would pass through. He had to take the bull by the horns.

"Señor Ramiro, can you just tell me where exactly you want the sign?"

"The third panel on the left from here."

Lucio engraved these words on his memory so as not to make a mistake. He counted: one, two, three. Then he glanced at Señor Ramiro, who was still standing, stern-faced and in profile, as if he were reviewing a regiment.

Lucio did his work neatly and skilfully. He carefully applied white paint to a stain in one corner of the panel, leaving it white and glossy. Then he picked up the ruler and took out a thick yellow pencil, which he wielded with consummate skill. The black sign, at the top on the left, was soon finished. Now he had to paint a firm, thick line, marked at intervals with red dots and with a larger red dot at the start of the line to indicate this station, the point of departure. As he was measuring the distance between the dots, he had a sudden moment of doubt. The train always arrives from the right, but where would this train be going? To Tetuán or to Sol? In one direction it called at six stations and in the other at four. He sidled over to Señor Ramiro.

"Excuse me, Señor Ramiro. I've just realized that you haven't told me if this is the train that goes to Sol or the other one."

Señor Ramiro stared at him hard and said:

"Well, I can't be expected to think of everything."

"I just need to know… because since there aren't any signs…"

"I thought you were the one providing the signs! It goes to Sol! Don't ask me again!"

The veins on Lucio's forehead stood out angrily and he turned away, muttering to himself. The one that goes to Sol. Lucio wrote it down in a notebook. However, when he reached the panel, he turned very pale, because he realized that he had yet another question. The line went from top to bottom, but should it start from the right or the left? He hurried back to the control booth to add this question to the previous one, so that they wouldn't appear to be two questions.

"I reckon the line should point that way."

"Good grief! I'm surprised you didn't bring your nursemaid with you!"

"Look, I don't see…"

"No, you *don't* see, do you?"

They fell silent. Señor Ramiro didn't say another word. Lucio felt like ramming his brush down Señor Ramiro's throat.

"You could at least provide some instructions."

"Oh, come on, boy! Don't you ever travel on the Metro?"

"Of course I do."

"So where does the train come in, from the right or from the left?"

"From the right of course. Where else?"

"Well, it's the same with the line you're painting! It goes from there to there!"

Lucio returned to his post in silence and continued his work. He'd had just about all he could take of this Ramiro guy, but when he'd finished, Señor Ramiro would soon change his tune. He spat emphatically onto the rails: Then they'll see what a proper painter can do!

A bell rang. A machineless silence fell, broken only by the dark, hidden voices approaching quietly but distinctly through the tunnel or along the passageways. Lights were turned off. Two workers walked silently past along the opposite platform. The "Ramiro guy" disappeared as well. The line Lucio had painted was straight as a die and he didn't intend to eat any lunch until he had finished. It was the first time he had worked in the Metro. It wasn't exactly a challenging job, but it was turning out pretty well.

He had jotted down in his notebook the names of the stations to Tetuán and to Sol. He underlined the ones going to Sol. And he knew the name of that particular station: Juan Navarro. A square with trees, old houses and a big public toilet with a double entrance for ladies and for gentlemen. That was the first name he put: Juan Navarro. There was no one around now who he could ask, and he had decided anyway not to bother with any more questions. He knew what he'd get: a blank look and a brusque, unhelpful answer. By the time he had applied the last brushstroke to the last name, he was feeling positively cheerful, after being alone for an hour and having a whole Metro station to himself in which he could whistle a happy tune. He had forgotten all about Señor Ramiro when he heard the bell ring again and saw him back at his post, saw the men pass by on the platform and heard the dull, blurred sound of hammer drills in the tunnel. His work was done, that was what mattered. The wall opposite hadn't been tiled yet and was still covered in peeling paint, the panels bare of plaster. Lucio had dealt with Señor Ramiro rather well, he thought; he'd done a good job and had the paint stains on his previously immaculate overalls to prove it. "Those who can, do; those who can't, give the orders. No, what was he saying? The one who gives the orders, judges, but doesn't give any actual orders at all. What help did Señor Ramiro give me?"

He picked up his things and went over to the control booth.

"Right, job done."

"Everything OK?"

"Yes."

"All finished?"

"Take a look."

Señor Ramiro did not move. He was immovable, confident, powerful.

"All finished?"

"Yes, all done."

"I'll take a look afterwards."

Lucio walked back across the plank to the other platform. He was tired of the noise, the dim, round, yellow lights and the dusty air. He was hungry too; well, it was three o'clock. He was not so much weary of the work as of Señor Ramiro. But at least he had done a good job. He'd like to see someone do it better. This thought cheered him, that and being able to go out into the clean air and the sunlight again, away from that great, stinking, cramped mousehole. Things look different in the light, he thought; you see everything more clearly, the birds sing, there are no mistakes, no doubts. In the light, everything is what it is and as it was. There's nothing else. You need to drag death and life out into the light, along with the stingy wages, your anger, as well as what happened now and what happened in the past. You have to take the risk of either evaporating like a drop of water or growing like a plant in the sun. You have to be like bits of cloth hung out to dry.

Lucio was dazzled by the light as he went up the first brightly lit stairs. Up above, he could see the leaves of a tree stirring. When he reached the square, he closed his eyes, then slowly opened them again. The large, docile sun hung dozing above the Earth. Lucio took a deep breath with his head up. His eyes fell on a blue plaque. "Plaza del General Pedro Navarro". Pedro, not Juan. Pedro. Pedro Navarro. He had put Juan. He stood stock still, not knowing what to do. Señor Ramiro had said: "I'll take a look afterwards." Did that mean now or later or tomorrow? When? Not that it made much difference. He smiled a slightly mischievous smile. "Oh, what the hell," he muttered.

There was a bar opposite and he went in.

"Give me a glass of wine, will you, Boni?"

THE CASHIER

W HEN SHE STARTED working at the bar, she was already past the first flush of youth. She had traipsed about her local neighbourhood, Legazpi, until her hips had grown spinsterish and sour, or, rather, soporific and slightly broad in the beam. Her boyfriend was also from the barrio, which had been witness both to her tears and her tear-smudged make-up. And when the relationship ended and she heard him say for the last time: "Look, sweetheart, let's call it a day, shall we?", she, in order to forget and make the time pass more easily, got a job in Argüelles, in a bar, which involved a long daily commute by tram or Metro; in short, she took up travelling.

Don Arcadio, the owner of the Café El Buen Suceso, gave the new cashier her instructions: Wear a black uniform with a nice clean white collar. Go to the bank on the corner every morning to get change for a thousand-peseta note. No fiddling the accounts and no chat. And if the till's a bit short, it'll be taken off your wages at the end of the month. Rosita Pascual said: Yes, sir, and then

64

went and sat down at the till, which was in a kind of recess set into the counter, facing the customers.

Initially, Rosita's large, dark, prominent eyes rolled and shifted about above the till, with the intention of looking cheerful and attractive. And when Manolín, the waiter, said, for example, "Four pesetas" and handed her a five-peseta piece, Rosita would give him the change, saying: "There you are." And later to the departing customer: "Goodbye, sir! Have a good day!" or "Goodbye, sir! Have a good evening!"

During the day, time after time, everyone, Manolín, Fabián the manager, Pepe and Antonio, Isabel and Ketty, would approach that recess in the counter to deposit the customers' money on the marble pedestal beneath the till or in Rosita Pascual's hard but ladylike hand. And Rosita, who had a keen eye for certain things, came to consider herself the very heart of the café and began to assert her authority. One morning, she said to the waiter: "Manolín, sweetheart, would you mind going to the bank to get some change?" And Manolín went. And over time, that phrase slowly mutated into: "Manolín didn't go to the bank this morning, the laggard." One day, she neglected to put on her regulation black uniform, and when Don Arcadio asked her about this, she said: "It's being washed, Don Arcadio, but this dark dress is just as discreet and just as nice, don't you agree?" And gradually, imperceptibly, the dark dress replaced the black uniform with the white collar and, in the end, the owner of the bar came round to the idea and said, Yes, it was fine. Then, on one occasion, she went to her boss's desk and said: "Look, Don Arcadio, I know you're not happy with Julita, the girl who does the other shift. I don't trust her either, to be honest; she's no good at adding up and the slightest thing confuses her. If you like, I could do both shifts. After all, there are always quiet times when I can take a rest." And so it was that Rosita Pascual became the sole cashier at the Café El Buen Suceso: weddings, christenings, coffees and spirits. Cashier and very nearly queen, for her head was crowned by two bottles of anis that stood on a little shelf behind her, Anís Morterito and Anís Rodrigo Vázquez, whose labels bore the pictures of two famous toreadors, facing each other like rivals in the ring.

The good thing about the till was that it reigned supreme over everything. Not only did all the money handled in the bar come there, but, at quiet times, all the employees' stories and financial worries came too, and sometimes the way in which these were relayed to her had a distinct whiff of the consulting room about them. The till was also a splendid observation post, from which, for example, one could watch the love of an old man for a young girl and another very different kind of love, over-ripe and insipid and past its best, and which only tends to be resolved once the man involved has belatedly passed the long-awaited exams required to get a better job; or one could observe the ideas and the worlds that some poor writer was tirelessly pursuing from his table, or the looks and gestures of the solitary woman and the solitary man, and from there, too, one could hear the grotesque, foul-mouthed voices of post-menopausal get-togethers and the fresh, fiery words of students.

For Rosita, the bar was a place where anything could happen, a music box full of surprises, with the advantage that she was inside that great music box and could subtly change the melody with just a glance or a word. In the mornings, the customers, drenched in light, seemed to Rosita to have a golden glow about them, they talked loudly and there hung in the air the aroma of those autumnal brown cigars that make one think of strong, swarthy men with money and expensive cars. In the afternoons, in the long hours until the lights were turned on, the customers changed in appearance, allowing themselves to be filled right down to the bottoms of their pockets with a glittering, greenish light, an aquarium light, like a sauce that eases the digestion and gently dissolves ideas. Then came the vulgar, ecstatic, dizzying hour of the young couples. And at night, the shrill yellow light, the yellow of funerals, liquorice root and brass cymbals, clung to the flesh of the various night owls and suspect couples, who emerged from the tunnel of night looking new and elastic, confident and free, and filled with a somewhat malign spirit.

The till recorded the sales and then, at the appropriate moment, automatically added them up, while Rosita tirelessly recorded the hidden depths and ways of the regular customers, dissecting their souls with a look and drawing conclusions and results whose truth she would put to the test by using the catalyst of a comment or a conversation.

One day, Don José, the odontologist, looked at Rosita. It was the look she had been waiting for, and Rosita began to look at Don José too. He was wearing a wedding ring, but this fact provoked in Rosita only relative unease. And it was this perhaps—so that there could be no possible room for doubt—that prompted Don José to turn up one afternoon at the Café El Buen Suceso with his lady wife and his three offspring in tow, plus one baby not yet weaned and still in the pram. The children clearly adored their papa. His lady wife ordered hot chocolate, cake, milk and anything else she fancied. Don José was clearly not alone. He had probably only looked at Rosita that once in order to appraise her teeth. As far as Rosita was concerned, Don José could look where he liked, although, truth be told, married men really had no right to look anywhere.

She was still sighing over these sad thoughts when she noticed, standing at one end of the bar, Isabel's boyfriend, who worked as a waiter at El Guayacán and who, as usual, was waiting for Isabel as he silently drank a coffee. Isabel was lucky. Isabel went over and spoke to him, said goodbye to Rosita and her other colleagues, and then she and her boyfriend went off together arm in arm.

It seems that another customer, Señor Quintana, was also in the habit of looking at her. She only looked at him on alternate days in order to make him jealous, but on the days when she did look at him, she positively besieged him with looks that were sometimes clear and impetuous and sometimes soft and insinuating. Señor Quintana, we should say, was a clerk of the court and when he first noticed Rosita looking at him, he immediately considered the moral consequences, but, on one occasion, was so far tempted that he found himself doing sums in his head to work out how much he could, at a pinch, afford per month. Señor Quintana, however, far from being an impulsive man, was the very soul of caution and didn't want to give up the café, or miss out on his cigar on Thursdays and Sundays, or delay work on the modest house he was having built in Pozuelo. Besides, Señor Quintana already had someone at home: his wife.

Rosita wasn't lucky like Isabel. Nor was she like Ketty, whom Don Ángel picked up each night at around one o'clock. Don Ángel was not her boyfriend, because boyfriends are never called Don anything. All that awaited Rosita, when the bar closed, were the shadows of the trees on moonlit nights, the last tram, the occasional drunken passer-by and the nightwatchman's sideways glances.

Until one day, the magnet of the cash register attracted the gaze of Don Andrés Llorente, a rentier and a gentleman, with a bad cough and a certain macho arrogance, who was getting on in years, perhaps too much so.

Don Andrés was a regular customer at El Buen Suceso. He talked about the law, because he had studied to be a lawyer, but he talked about medicine too, because he had a nephew who was an eminent doctor, and about architecture, politics and business, because he had relatives involved in those areas too. He spoke in such virile tones that the veins on his forehead stood out. He was a proper man. He used to visit the bar before lunch for an aperitif and in the evening, at eight o'clock, he would wait in a corner of the café for the arrival of a modest young girl, with whom he would talk very quietly, opening and closing his eyes a great deal and making large gestures. The young woman would sometimes laugh as if she were at the circus. And sometimes she would be heard to cry in a shrill, rather vulgar voice:

"Ooh, Andrés, the things you say!"

Then, one evening, she did not come.

"I say, Manolín, has my niece been in?"

And Rosita seized the opportunity to ask:

"Oh, is she a relative of yours, the young woman you meet here?"

Very gravely, carefully composing his features and modulating his voice, Don Andrés spoke rather loftily about that common misfortune, common at least in the upper classes: divorce. A brother of his had frittered away a fortune, married badly, and now his poor children were paying for his mistakes. The girl who met him in the café was one of his brother's daughters, the eldest; he sometimes gave her money and was trying to find her a job. "Well, it's hardly the poor little angel's fault," said Don Andrés wisely and with unusual restraint.

"Ah, the things that life throws at us!" sighed Rosita. "It's lucky for them that they have such a kind uncle who can help them out a little."

"Who did you think she was, then? No, I like mature women like yourself, the kind of woman who, when you get up close, gives off the sound of the sea, just like pressing your ear to a seashell."

When he wasn't coughing, Don Andrés was quite silver-tongued and made remarkably eloquent use of his hat in conversation. To Rosita—even though she had no idea whether he was a bachelor or not—he seemed like a man idealized by bachelordom and capable of being as obedient as a schoolboy, a man who would meekly allow someone to tend his various coughs and colds. Gradually, the niece—the supposed niece, thought Rosita to herself—began to visit the café less often and, in the end, stopped coming altogether; indeed, on the last few occasions, she had argued with Don Andrés and been rude to him. Day by day, Don Andrés and Rosita exchanged more and more comments and confidences, and Rosa frequently left the cash register to go over to the bar, like a young girl going to the street window to trade sweet nothings with her lover. He was in no hurry to sin; his body now had little to do with his words and remained slightly aloof, waiting its turn, always alleging aches and pains and other pretexts. They had spent many days now embroiled in sad, delicate family histories, which embellish and lend a sheen of unhappiness to both eyes and skin. Rosita was not happy. Don Andrés—ah, what a falling-off had there been—now lacked the very dearest of affections. The world, he said, was full of ungrateful people.

"I just can't believe they would do that to you, Don Andrés!"

And he, tactfully, said no more, so as not to pour more poison into what he imagined to be Rosita's innocent soul.

"Oh, the tales I could tell you… Then you'd know what it is to be a man."

And they agreed that she would reduce her working day to just one shift so that they could meet somewhere else at a decent hour, because being able to talk as freely as they did was really something very special.

And so that is what they agreed, and it was then that the newspapers starting trumpeting forth in banner headlines the arrival of a fast-moving cold front accompanied by strong winds. And the cold front duly arrived, setting the geography shivering, sending goose pimples throughout all Iberia and carrying off with it Don Andrés, that very proper husk of a man, full of impure hopes and terrible memories. It happened rather suddenly. As if death had finally taken seriously his many lamentations, not realizing that they were only the measure of the affection he was asking of Rosita. And so off Don Andrés went. Along with four cows in Lugo, an old lady in Ávila, a truck carrying flour in Soria, a nightwatchman in La Felguera, a little boy in Peñarroya and another in Sama de Langreo.

Rosita, now the grieving widow of a plan, exalted their story and filled the memory of their friendship with sudden, gentle floods of tears, with melancholy and respect. She continued to work all day in the café. At night, when it closed, and the figures of Morterito and Rodrigo Vázquez were left alone to stick their tongues out at each other, what awaited Rosita now were not only the shadows of the trees on moonlit nights, but also another friendlier, less noticeable shadow, one that smelt of cigarettes and coffee, had the sparkle of a diamond ring and walked with the small, delicate steps of a gentleman: the shadow of Don Andrés Llorente, ill-fated lover and the broken handle through which Rosita Pascual had once, God willing, hoped to slip her quiet, plump, anodyne arm.

THE ALBUM

T HEY HURRIED into the café and sat down. Their eyes were bright with impatience as they placed the package on the table. She had barely taken her place there when she began to open the package, gazing lovingly first at the red ribbon used to tie up the package and then, with a kind of protective, expectant pride, at his face.

"What can I get you?" asked the waiter.

"I'll have a white coffee. What about you?"

"The same."

On the table, in its navy-blue covers, like someone's Sunday-best suit of clothes, was the album of picture cards. This was a great day. They had talked about it as one might talk about the birth of a child. The album represented the young man's childhood tenacity, which had collected one picture card after another until all the landscapeless windows of that difficult book were filled. His schoolmates—he recalled—had left empty spaces of indifference and idleness in their albums. His, resplendent on the table, revealed the devotion, in its day, of a careful man, who had remained faithful all his life to his most innocent joys, to the object of his most insignificant enthusiasm. For his girlfriend, that blue album symbolized perseverance and constancy. There, on the table, was the white coffee of their humble love, but there, too, inside the book, were all the marvels of the universe, from which they began slowly, lovingly, to pull off the petals, as if their happiness, a Yes or a No, depended upon the answer.

"No," she said gleefully, "not 'The Butterflies' today. And we've done 'The Great Inventions'."

Each page drew them closer together, day after day. On the day of 'The Butterflies', she had fluttered her eyelashes at a young man sitting opposite, and he—the boyfriend—had felt jealous. But she hadn't, in fact, even looked at that other man; she had simply wanted to flutter her own fine eyelashes like a butterfly. On the day of 'Domestic Birds', they imagined the home they would have along with an orange canary sitting bright and almost transparent in the sunny window: "White would be better," he suggested. "No, it has to be orange," she said firmly, screwing up her eyes as if wincing at the bird's bittersweet plumage. The 'Exotic Birds' page placed a daring little hat of gaudy feathers gently on her head, on an afternoon in which the world would be full of laughter, champagne and confetti. On the day of 'Flowers for Giving', he gave her a bouquet of twelve tulips so that she would not forget a shared moment. When they reached 'Prehistoric Animals', she felt afraid and they moved still closer. He was keen to spend a few more days studying those 'Prehistoric Animals', but she refused and hurried on to the glittering pages of 'Precious Stones', which, for atavistic reasons, filled him with unease and suspicion. He saw in her eyes a certain courtly brazenness, certain boundless ambitions, which made him feel uncomfortable all afternoon and placed between them a clammy, amphibian coldness. When they came to 'Algae', they entwined fingers, hands, arms, looks and words. They had a splendid time with 'The Evolution of the Motorcar', bouncing up and down on their seats and juddering to a halt. She identified so closely with the 'Wild Animals' that her eyes filled up with predatory instinct and he felt like a tragic lion-tamer who might perish at any moment. With 'Fauna of the Sea', the sweet, idle, gentle fishes of love swam back and forth from her eyes to his and continued to do so, meekly, humbly, the whole afternoon. When they came to 'Fruit', she blushed and placed one hand over the apples to stop in their tracks any progressive Adam-like thoughts.

They finished the album and were left tanned and exhilarated as after a long journey. It was as if they had returned with the same shared memories from a respectful honeymoon. She waited every day—especially the last one—for him to say: "Here, take it, this album is for you." But he didn't. Filling that album with picture cards had been his childhood joy; it had made him a prize exhibit whenever they had visitors. And so he took his album and kept it. If he had given it to her, she would have returned his gift in words full of understanding and colour, in experience of the world, in botanical beauties and ocean deeps. But the afternoons grew colder and both of them grew bored; they choked on their now broken words. And one day, she—who had fallen in love with the album—said goodbye. When the time comes, he will have to get the album out again, but without ever daring to give it away.

THE LEMON DROP

I'M STANDING AT THE DOOR of the house where Cobos' wife lives. The wife of Ramiro Cobos, retired quartermaster-general in the air force. He'd be a hero if it wasn't for that word "quartermaster". It's two o'clock. The sun is beating down, and the people—not many at this hour—are hurrying home for lunch. I feel tired. On other days, it's been after three o'clock and yet I've never before felt this tightness around my waist, this weight in my legs—especially in my feet—and this complete and utter inertia, yes, that too. It's really muggy, one of those hot, heavy days. I look at my suitcase; well, I call it a suitcase, but it's not that big, more of a briefcase really, and, as always, I have a quick peek inside to make sure nothing's missing. The briefcase weighs on me too; it's hot, it's had enough, it's about ready to explode, as if it contained some deadly substance. But it doesn't. Or perhaps it does; I'm not sure. It contains my life, which isn't deadly exactly, but it is mortal. Lace edgings, doilies, buttons, ribbons, thread, handkerchiefs. Froth. That's what I sell: froth. And I probably won't ever sell anything else.

It's hard work getting Señora Cobos to buy anything. After an hour of chat—amiable, exhausting chat—she can't even bring herself to part with ten pesetas. It's a sheer waste of time. It makes my brain and my tongue ooze honey, filling every part of me with mellifluous words that upset my stomach and possibly my mood too.

Yes, we're both of us tired, the briefcase and me. The briefcase, poor thing, nudged me in the leg and, without even realizing, we set off homewards.

Did the morning turn out well or badly? I don't really know. Not that it matters. What really seems to matter is that the morning turned out one way or another—for someone else, of course. It doesn't belong to me anyway. It never has. The morning belongs to that important gentleman, Work, who has shares in every one of us. But that's all right. And chatting—even to myself—has always come easily to me. The thing is that I now have, let's see, seventy, no, eighty-two pesetas in my pocket. They're not mine either. You have to subtract the boss's percentage first. Quite a large percentage. The only mathematical operation I know how to perform is subtraction. Mathematics for me consists of subtracting a certain percentage. Mathematics—how many years ago is it now?—was my father's obsession. "Learn calculus, arithmetic and accounting!" he used to say. My poor father! Despite the moustache, the big, bony hands and the rather coarse voice, he had the face of someone who was good with numbers!

Shall I go down this street? The Mora family live just around the corner. No. I'll go this way today and pop round some other time to see what's what.

If someone had told me I was going to live this life of doorbells and stairways, of brisk commerce and a brief-case full of froth, of playing the friendly pedlar from nine to five, I would never have believed them. Never. When I was a boy, I used to go bird's-nesting and I had scabby knees. I used to smoke on the sly. Now I never smoke. I used to own a pellet gun. I have big hands, like cowboys in the Wild West. And by "I", I mean this person who is me. This weary fellow who walks home bent beneath the weight of his briefcase, which, one day, grabbed hold of his hand like a dog and feels equally weary.

I think I must be slightly feverish. My mouth is dry. Probably from talking all that time with Señora Cobos or else from the heat. After something sweet, after honey, you need a drink of water.

"Afternoon, old girl! Give me three of those sweets, will you?"

Will they ever finish mending this road?

When I think about it, I haven't bought any sweets in ages. They're expensive though. Three sweets, one peseta fifty. A bit pricey, I reckon. Kids these days have money though. Or maybe these atomic-age children don't eat sweets. Hmm. I expect that, proportionally, boys now have more money than us men. Most boys would have fifty centavos to buy themselves a sweet. And yet how hard a grown man has to work to accumulate forty times those fifty centavos. That's all some men earn in a day. Twenty pesetas and a wife and children to support, because children are inevitable when all you have is a wife and no money. I have it pretty easy, really.

Yes, I must be feverish. I'm so hot. That's all we need, for me to get ill as well. The two of us in bed. I've probably caught a chill. I'll drink a glass of milk and brandy. A good glassful. But I'd better not say anything to Pili. No, I'm just tired; that's all.

I'm really pleased I bought those sweets, though. Once you're a grown-up, you tend not to buy them any more, as if they were for children only, and so we never again gaze with greedy wonder at the green or pink or yellow or red of a big boiled sweet. To boys, a sweet is like a temptation from their little inner devil, just as a neighbour's beautiful, virtuous wife is for men. The old lady who sold them to me was very neat and well turned out, and she wore a white oversleeve on her right arm, like those women who sell curd cheese. Or like a confectioner. Not that the sleeve will be of much use to her. She probably assumed I was buying the sweets for my kids. But no, there are no kids, Señora. They're all for me. I said: "Afternoon, old girl! Give me three of those sweets, will you?" And

I struck lucky, just as if I'd won the lucky dip, a cherry one, a strawberry one and a lemon one. Each in its own paper wrapper bearing a picture of the corresponding fruit, juicy, ripe and scented. Now that's what I call a sweet, the sort that fills your cheek and does battle with your teeth and floods your mouth with juice. Not the silent, sticky sort, that lingers on your molars like a slow fox trot, a sickly sweet nightmare, a friend to tooth decay. This strawberry one's really good. And it's cheaper than a beer. My daily beer at the Florida is in grave danger, I fear. I'm travelling back now into the old world of boiled sweets. They contain sugar and carbohydrates, which are, apparently, essential to a healthy diet, or so I read in the *Reader's Digest*. My daily glass of beer is getting to be something of an extravagance. I mean, before you know it, the money's gone.

"Good afternoon!"

I've no idea who that gentleman is. Neither has Pili. I asked her once and she said she didn't know. He's obviously confused me with someone else, but we always say hello. Still, it's nice to know people. One day, he'll stop greeting me. When he meets the other man, the one he thinks he's saying hello to, the one he really does know. Or perhaps he's just one of those friendly types who says hello to everyone. And why not? It's not a bad way to get through life.

"Hi, Julia!"

Now I do know who she is. She's the concierge. She rushes out, goes up the steps and opens the lift door for me. As she always does. It's a modest house, but at least we have a lift. And gas on every floor. The lift is slow, of course. It's a fairly rickety affair and noisy too. The buttons for the different floors are red. You can tell at once that it would have preferred to serve a different class of person and that it's not happy here. Passing, as it does, people's kitchen windows, it smells of fried food, and, on the roof, there are sometimes even discarded fish bones coated in dust and the ignominious curls of potato peelings. It's a sad lift, going up and down all day, with no velvet walls and no seat.

I wonder if Pili's feeling better. It's the usual problem: pains around the waist, something to do with her ovaries. And she said her throat felt tight today too. Yes, this morning, when I looked, I thought I could see a small white mark on the left side. A spot. She's probably been up dusting and cleaning the whole apartment. I sometimes think she's a bit obsessive about housework. Often, when I come home, she makes me walk on the newspapers she's put down in the corridor so that I don't dirty the floor. At first, I tried to convince her that a corridor isn't a paten or a mirror or a plate, but a path, the path you find in all apartments, one that you have to walk down in order to go from room to room. That was in the early days. I've long since given up trying.

Ah, I forgot to press the button to send the lift back down. There she is, yes, there she is, the nosy parker opposite, peering through the spyhole in her front door. It's an odd thing, education. An educated person living in a world not his own—as is my case—is a person without hope. Unless, one day, I simply crack.

Right, have you had a good look at me? May I close my door now? If you haven't had your fill, I can wait a little longer. Right, I'm sorry, that's enough. If you'll excuse me. Dreadful woman!

"Pili!"

The poor thing doesn't look at all well.

"Do you want some water? Wait a moment."

I go into the kitchen. There are four dirty pots in the sink. She must be feeling bad.

"Pilar! Piluca! Pilarín! You're not well. You look really tired. Go to sleep. Don't you worry about me. Of course, I know, but don't worry. I know where everything is. I can sort myself out. I'll find it. Yes, I know, first the fish and then the meat. And the salad. It's so hot outside. You're fine here in the bedroom, though, with the window open a bit; it's much cooler."

It's going to be like last time. She really is in a bad way.

The fish! Let's eat something. Here it is. It doesn't look too fresh. It has a bit of a whiff about it, a smell that's too penetrating, maternal somehow, almost sour. I can't find the bread, but it doesn't matter. No, it doesn't matter, but finding the bread is, in fact, crucial. If Pili knew I was eating a meal without bread, she'd be out of that bed like a shot. I'll have a snack later, around seven.

Now for the meat. And the salad. The meat tastes of nothing. It's like chewing a piece of gum. It's an exhausted piece of meat that's left all its juice and colour and savour on the butcher's marble slab. A piece of meat that deserves to be left in peace and given a decent burial. Chewing it actually leaves a bad taste in the mouth. I don't know why, and I'm surprised really, but it does. And I don't like the salad either. It's green and bitter and sad. Too much brilliantine on its curls, I reckon. What a shame! It's brought tears to my eyes. Must be the sight of all that greenery.

There's a flake of soot on the edge of my plate. It must have blown in through the window from the courtyard. What this table needs is bread and, above all, it needs Pili.

Why are you ill, Pili? What's wrong? What is the name of your illness? Where does it hurt you?

Pili is ill. It's nothing serious. It will pass. But the illness hangs around nonetheless and turns up another day. And she obeys the illness and goes to bed. She obeys the mystery. It's as if the word "woman" bruised her body. Perhaps Pili isn't just ill occasionally, perhaps she's permanently ill, perhaps I married a sick woman.

"I brought you a sweet, Pilarín. Here, you choose. The cherry one? All right. That leaves me with the lemon drop. I'm going to keep you company, here on the camp bed. I won't talk. I feel a bit tired myself."

The camp bed. I sleep here some nights, when she's not well. When you're married, it's quite a privilege to have a camp bed all to yourself. I didn't like it at first. But now it's my old and faithful friend, and I feel free when I lie down on it, very free, like a lone sailor. I enjoy having a camp bed, leaving my wife to set sail on the double bed.

It's really pretty, this sweet paper. Cheerful. I like looking at it, and it seems a shame to just scrunch its colours up in my hand. On one side, near the edge, there's a lemon tree out of which springs, into the very centre of the wrapper, a ripe yellow lemon, framed by green leaves and a white flower. Yellow and green. Yellow, green and white. The taste of this lemon drop has something to tell me. It's about to speak. As if the taste, years ago, on a certain day, was already there, locked up in time; a day that this sour, lemon-flavoured saliva is seeping back into in order for it to be filled with light and discovered anew. My saliva slides into my body, sour and hot, and reaches a point where a long-lost picture suddenly lights up, a corner that, for years now, has been waiting for this viscous rain to allow it to remember. It's as if a bubble from the lemon drop had set the bubbles in a glass of lemonade fizzing. And all it takes for everything to fill with sunlight is this sharp, sour ache in my jaw and

the accompanying yelp of delight from my taste buds.
And my nerves spring into action and my brain busily
furnishes the memory stored away in my memory bank
with the necessary information.

A long morning in the village, with the smell of food
scorching the air, which, perfumed with stews, warms
the earth and the paving stones and the grains of wheat
in the cracks in between. Soap. Mass. Posters. Women's
scent wafting along the pavement, the cigarette smoke
from the men standing on the corner, breathing out a
breath of sadness at the passing children. Short trousers
with creases as stiff and straight as a pencil and very tight
behind, and my party shoes gnawing at my heels like a
little dog. Creases. Wet hair that continued to drip all the
way down Calle Realejo de San Juan. Laura. Yes, now I
remember what happened with Laura. I never wanted to
do it; it made me sad. She would close the blinds and get
dressed in the dark of her bedroom. She would kiss me
and squeeze me and rub me against her legs, then open
the window and start combing my hair. And afterwards,
in the kitchen, she would melt some wax for me over the
heat and make a ball of it for me to play with.

One day, a lady arrived. My mother said she was her
niece. My mother had nieces who weren't my cousins.
She would adopt them when we went to the seaside or
on some trip or other. "No, he hasn't been a good boy
today," my mother said. "Don't give him anything."

Although it wasn't true. I was sure that I had been good, but then I would remember Laura, and a watery knot of grief would rise from my throat to my eyes, and two tears, the tears of a condemned man, would moisten my eyelashes or run down my cheeks onto the floor. She smiled, my mother's niece. She was pleased to see me. She liked me, even though I had just emerged, pale with fear, crumpled and sad, from Laura's inexplicable bedroom. She had a really beautiful mouth. Afterwards, I would often stand alone in front of a mirror, imitating her mouth, her expression, trying to copy that charming click of the tongue she made whenever she laughed over certain words. She opened her bag. She gave me a sweet. That sweet burned my mouth with its juice and filled my small body with oversize dreams. I was a little devil, my mother often used to say. But she never suspected that I was a reluctant devil to Laura and a semi-divine, redeemed and loving devil to her niece. When the niece opened her handbag, it gave a perfumed sigh. The same perfume she left on my hand. The hand that, later on, I did not wash before sitting down to lunch. How long did these things go on for, I wonder? I haven't seen her since. Or perhaps I have. Was she Amalita, perhaps? No, more likely a sister of hers. I remember Amalita really well. I was fourteen or fifteen by then.

When the other thing happened, the visit and the sweet, I was still a child. What I remember from that time are the days when there were bullfights. Perhaps there was a bullfight on the day of that visit, perhaps that was why she came. We used to go to my grandmother's house, which was in the same street as the bullring, to watch the people going past. An hour before the bullfight, the street smelt of blood, cigars, sweat and horse dung. I used to like going and standing on the balcony that looked out over the courtyard where the women did their ironing, because my mother's shouts took longer to reach me there. Did I perhaps feel that my mother was getting on a bit? Later, I would hear my father downstairs, loudly praising Armillita's skills as *banderillero*, imitating Cayetano going in for the kill or giving his views on Juan Belmonte's latest bulls. And the afternoon would be fading, and the last swallow would leave and the first bat arrive, and slowly, very slowly, the metal clothes lines out in the courtyard would grow cold.

The lemon drop! Gone all too soon. And yet the mystery remains. And I really can't say why it stirred so many memories. I revisited a world that, afterwards, I left behind for ever. Wasn't I the boy who was going to write *Paradise Lost* or *The Divine Comedy*? Something very valuable was cut short. And something perhaps far more ordinary was set in motion.

There's probably a sweet somewhere that would remind us of our wedding night and one that would take us back to the Christmas when we won the lottery and the one that would make us relive the happy week when we were about to be made head of personnel.

If Pilarín knew what I was thinking… But I won't tell her. I feel as if I've been unfaithful to her with that lemon drop. No, I'm not well. I just wish I could sleep.

THAT NOVEL

LUIS IS AN HONEST LAD, with arms strong enough to lift just about any piece of luggage onto a roof rack or help out the mechanics or force open a jammed door or pick up an old lady, however fat and ungainly, and either heave her onto the bus or save her from falling. Luis inspires confidence; he has a clear, clean, honest laugh; his arms exude human warmth and sweat. "I lost my mother when I was only three," I told him once, quite why I don't know. His eyes misted up and he had to go and sit in a corner to hide his tears. He still has his mother and his sisters and wouldn't hesitate to use his fists on anyone who harmed them. He's an ordinary lad, but extraordinary too, graced with old-fashioned moral notions, with the kind of simple beliefs and affections that have always made life more pleasant. He's a bright lad, and anyone who's ever had anything to do with him would always want the best for him: a decent boss, good luck, happiness and success, and the chance to make his mark on the world.

I would never have thought any of this if it weren't

for the fact that I'm about to leave him. Because there's one unusual thing about Luis. Well, I've always thought it unusual. First, I should say that I've been working for La Campurriana for the last three years and I'm now moving to a bigger firm. Perhaps I'll be able to persuade them to take Luis on too.

The buses leave first thing in the morning and then after five o'clock in the afternoon. At four, I open the ticket office, and Luis, once he's raised the metal shutter, sits around waiting or studying the stained and crumpled page from some old newspaper that's been used as wrapping paper. And time passes. He doesn't actually read the page. He just studies it, turns it over, yawns and, sometimes, takes a closer look at an article or photo that, for some reason, attracts his attention. Then he drops it on the floor, takes out a cigarette, looks across at me and, after that, we usually exchange a few words and chat away until five o'clock.

We talk about all kinds of things. For example, the new bus that the boss has been promising us for over a year and which never arrives, and which I won't see now because I'm leaving. Or how many passengers could you fit into the old Chevrolet—was it only sixteen or more? The cute girl who caught the bus to Los Molinos yesterday. The continuing feud between Paco and Manolo, who are the company's longest-serving employees. The fair in San Sebastián de los Reyes, Valdemorillo or Navalcarnero.

Whether business is going well or badly. The cold or the heat. Whether the boss will treat us to a celebratory chicken supper on 18 July again. How Matías, the new boy, isn't a bad little flamenco singer. How Manolo has been saying that the fields are crying out for water. And how, according to Paco, the rain has ruined the crops.

Anyway, at some point in the conversation, Luis almost always gives a little smile, raises his eyebrows, stares down at his knees and says: "I read a novel once…"

Let me explain. Some topic always crops up, whether to do with the company or with something else entirely, something that reminds Luis of that novel he read. In the last three years, I don't think we've talked about anything important, or unimportant, that Luis hasn't already found—in richer, livelier, more memorable form—in that novel. Be it fishing, hunting, football, theatre, cinema, the pools, monsters; millionaires, the poor, politicians, tombolas; war and peace; the unfortunate, the fortunate, gamblers, women, adventurers, historical figures; the concierge at No. 54; Algeria, Germany, North America, Russia, Spain; the Galicians, the Catalans, the illiterate, teachers, maids, aristocrats, office workers, businessmen, horses, greyhounds, tigers, lions, aircraft, ships, motorbikes, cars, trains, villages, cities; the moon, space, the sea, the land; volcanoes; marriage, apartments; the lottery, the radio; priests, fathers, sons, bullfighters, soldiers, our fellow countrymen in general.

Whenever there was a pause while Luis rummaged around in his memory before saying: "I read a novel once", the air would grow dense, would stop to listen, and the faded orange paint on the partition walls that separate us from the public—and which smell of madeleines, grease, white bread, baskets of figs and, for some strange reason, when it rains, of fresh printer's ink—would grow somehow brighter, because there, in that novel, was the very thing we were talking about, only better, loftier, more poignant and full of unforgettable feeling, interest and detail.

I've often thought that the book must have been *Don Quixote*, but then I decided it couldn't be, because, whatever they may say, *Don Quixote* isn't much read outside of schools, perhaps because it's too good. I haven't read it myself. And I can't imagine Luis reading it. At other times, I thought it might be a detective novel or an adventure story, but people who know about these things never read such books and presumably with good reason. I suppose, basically, they're always the same; there's a plot, sure, but they're really just a way of passing the time, books to be read on the Metro. In the last three years, I've come up with all kinds of possibilities: Salgari, for example, or Jules Verne, although he wrote mainly fantasy stuff. Or Zane Grey or James Oliver Curwood. For a long time I thought it might be Blasco Ibáñez, because his books are a bit meatier and he's almost as famous as Di Stefano

the footballer. But Blasco Ibáñez, it seems, spoke out of
turn, and his work is pretty much ignored now. That's
what Jaime the Valencian told me anyway, and it's true
that nowadays you almost never hear his name even
mentioned. So perhaps it was Blasco Ibáñez. I don't know.
Although a novel like the one that Luis once read could
really only have been written by God.

I've read a fair bit myself, and it's true that every now
and then I've read a novel I simply couldn't put down,
but I've still never come across anything like Luis' novel,
in which he saw and experienced everything just that
bit more intensely than other people. It's never far from
his mind. I've sometimes wondered why he's never read
anything else, having been so lucky that once; or perhaps
he thought it was so marvellous precisely because it was
the only novel he'd read. Or perhaps he tried reading
other books, but was disappointed. I've also suspected
that it's out of sheer modesty that Luis attributes to that
novel all the good things he thinks, imagines or feels.
Because he never goes any further. He says: "I read a
novel once…", then smiles, stares down at his knees or
into the distance, makes a vague, contented gesture, as
if to say: "Need I go on?" And the subject is dropped
or, rather, it continues to grow in the silence, and we, or
at least I, feel diminished, embarrassed, bereft, because
I haven't read that novel or a novel like it, and I'm
left waiting for something more, something that never

comes. And I always forget to ask the question I most want to ask.

But I didn't want to leave La Campurriana without asking him: "Luis, what novel was it that you read? What was it called? Who wrote it?" Today—my last day here—I asked him several times. But he couldn't remember.

RESTLESS EYES

H E COULD HEAR ONLY the sound of running water in the bathroom. He was sitting by the window in an old rocking chair, reading the newspaper. Now and then, he gazed absently out at the sky and yawned. The soft glow of evening reached as far as the corridor. A light was on in a bedroom inside the apartment. It had been on for more than an hour—a soft, tenuous light, as if from a bedside lamp. He heard the bathroom door close and, shortly afterwards, the sound of water filling the bath stopped. Now he could hear gentle splashings and tricklings and soapy cascadings. He folded up the newspaper and placed it on his knees. He yawned again and glanced up at a calendar on the wall: Saturday, 5 April. He closed his eyes and fell instantly asleep. The newspaper gradually slid off his lap and onto the floor.

When the light came on, he opened his eyes.

"I must have fallen asleep," he murmured, rubbing his face with one hand and stretching slightly.

Then he picked up the newspaper, tossed it onto the table, got to his feet and lowered the blind; then, drawing the rocking chair closer to the table and the light, he sat down again and began to read the back page.

"So, what do you say? Shall we have supper?" she said, leaning in the doorway, her hair caught up on the top of her head, her freshly washed body wrapped in a soft, clinging bathrobe.

"Yes, if you like," he answered, his words distorted by another long yawn.

She came into the room and lowered the blind properly. A few of the slats hadn't quite closed. Then she turned on the radio and waited, bending her head towards it and looking up, until the distant, burbling thread of a trite little tune and a presenter's voice made themselves heard and immediately filled the whole room. She carefully tamed the voice until it was warm and gentle, like a familiar caress, like the slow, soft touch of bathwater on thighs. The sharp, wild, blithe music of Saturday—the music of the Saturday-night variety programmes—brought the apartment back to life.

Now, intermittently, beneath the music, he could hear the clatter of pots and pans in the kitchen, drawers opening and closing, the occasional sudden gush of water in the sink or a chair briefly scraping the floor. And, all the while, the Saturday melody was filling the shadowy corners of the apartment like a long, silent, surreptitious puff of smoke.

They sat down to eat.

"Do you know, I dozed off."

"Don't you recognize this music?" she said, looking up at a point above his head. Her face brightened and she smiled slightly: "It's the music your nephew, Roberto, used to like."

"What do you mean *my* nephew? Isn't he your nephew too?"

"It's nice. Jones Farducci played it on the guitar in that film... oh, what was it called now?"

"I don't know," he said, using his fingers to remove a bit of bone from his mouth.

"Yes, you do. That film... *Six Men Shoot to Kill*. We saw it one Saturday. You never remember anything."

"That's your job. Anyway, did you have a good bath?"

"Yes, lovely. You could have had one too."

"Tomorrow."

"I like this presenter," she said suddenly. "He has a jokey, friendly way of speaking. By the way, have you got the tickets?" she asked, looking gratefully at the radio, as if flirting a little with the presenter.

"Yes, of course. Don't worry," she heard her husband's voice say beside her.

"So what are we going to see?" she said, delicately using her fork to manoeuvre a bit of gristle to the edge of the plate.

"The one you wanted to see... you know... oh, what's it called?"

"*The Moon Girls*?"

"That's it. I've no idea what it'll be like."

"We'll find out," she said, getting up.

She tidied the kitchen, went first into the dressing room and then into the bedroom. He returned to the rocking chair and opened the paper again. The waves of music drowned out the faint sounds of things being fastened, the silken rustle of fabric, the slight click of fingernail on button, the secret carnal whisper of an experienced hand smoothing a stocking. He heard, unhurried and sharp, the tap-tap of heels. Then she appeared at the dining-room door.

"Shall we go?"

He got lethargically to his feet and went into the bathroom, where he gave his hair a quick comb, and put on his jacket. On the stairs, as they went down, her footsteps sounded like the hoof-beats of a half-broken mare, nervous, on heat. The click-clack of her heels. He followed behind.

A light, scented breeze was ruffling the trees in the little square at the bottom of the street. Across the way, lights were on in almost every window.

"What time is it?"

"It's… oh, no, my watch has stopped."

"Trust you! Well, if we do have time, we can pop into Café Oms for a drink. And you can buy some cigarettes. It's on our way."

"OK."

Without looking at him, she slipped her arm through his, and they walked the two blocks to the Cine Gladis in silence. The streets were full of a perceptible nervous excitement, and the soft breeze from the acacias gently brushed the skin of passers-by.

"Shall we go in?… Except that, first, you need to find out what time it is!"

He asked a man who happened to be passing. It was half past ten. He stopped to put his watch right.

The café was crowded and noisy, heaving with people, and the waiter walked past them again and again with his tray full of drinks. A constant clink of glasses, plates and spoons came from behind the bar, and, from where they were standing, they could catch a strong whiff of coffee.

"Coffee with a dash for me," he said.

"And a black coffee for me."

"Do you want anything else to drink?"

"All right. I'll have one if you're having one."

People were already going into the cinema. The tall, meek, somewhat bored doormen in their brown uniforms were allowing the public through in dribs and drabs. The cinema smelt of disinfectant camouflaged by a thick, cloying perfume. "Icecreamsgetyouricecreamshere!" cried a young lad standing at the front. There was a burst of music, loud at first, then soft and melodic, reaching into every velvety corner, as the people padded across the carpets, talking in slightly hushed tones.

She occasionally spoke to him while they waited, but still without looking at him, without seeing him. She was speaking to a largish shape with the faculty of hearing, but who was an obstacle to her eyes—looking sometimes to the left and sometimes to the right—an obstacle that always prevented her physically or psychologically from seeing farther, seeing other things. She had grown used to talking to him. She barely turned her head when she did so. Her neck remained erect, strong, flexible, and full of pretty little shadows beneath the dark, silky locks of her hair.

"Isn't that the couple who live on the third floor? Yes, it is."

"It's nice this music, isn't it?"

As the lights went down, he said:

"Well, let's see what *The Moon Girls* have to offer!"

The subject of the film was a group of bored young women, disillusioned with life, who volunteer to fly rockets to the moon. They enter a secret military training base that specializes in space experiments, and where some equally bored and disillusioned young men are being trained for the same purpose. They have to submit to a regime of harsh discipline, but otherwise they have everything they need and a certain degree of comfort. The young men and women eye each other with about as much interest as if they were viewing a line of telegraph poles. In the bar, they exchange jaundiced views, all the while regarding each other with something approaching distaste and utter indifference. However, the healthy lifestyle and rigid routine, the lack of time to think, triggers in each of them a rebirth of strength, optimism and an incipient, ever-growing fear that they may die during the experiment. Three couples become romantically attached and get up to all kinds of adventures in their attempts to thwart the commanding officer's ban on them leaving the camp to get married. Their officers, cornered and sweating, finally succumb to the exigencies of love. So filled with regret are they that they promise to give the brides away on their wedding day and afterwards provide them all with safe posts at the base. The film ends at the door of the church, with everyone happy and smiling beneath a rain of rice. The moon smiles dotingly down at them. Meanwhile, back at the base, a beggar who has been hanging around the camp is being signed up as a crew member and, happily chewing on a hunk of stale bread, strides over to the rocket, takes a seat in the cabin and starts merrily pressing all the buttons, meanwhile beaming at the audience.

They filed slowly out of the cinema.

"It wasn't too bad, I suppose. A bit daft though," he said, stringing out the words on a long yawn.

She was walking slowly along, not talking. Films made her silent. She was listening to what the people behind them were saying. She paused calmly to wait for a car approaching in the distance to pass. As she walked, she stretched her legs with a kind of grave elegance, assured, measured, supple, suggestive of an attractive, inward-turned, mature indifference. She could hear the murmured conversations of various groups of people as they set off down side streets or parted company with friends. Others were strolling unhurriedly towards the Metro. She was filled by a pleasant sensation, by the playful, flickering flame of a vague desire, the savour of a different world, a world of carefree, amusing people, who spouted clever nonsense while gazing lovingly at each other and whose only thought was to kiss and dance and defeat death at all costs. Of all the characters, she had taken a particular fancy to John, a gawky figure with a child's eyes and cheerful canine teeth!

They reached their street, lit by the cool, silent moon. A cat crossed her path, proud, alert, noiseless. Behind her, in the distance, she heard the lone, echoing footsteps of a man, young, confident, slow, scything a path along the startled pavement. The steps were getting nearer. They sounded closer now. She thought: "That's how the actor, that cheeky fellow John must walk in real life. I wonder what his name is."

They reached their building.

"Here we are!"

She went in and, while he was turning the key in the lock, she grasped the grille on the heavy street door, as if waiting for him to finish. The man following behind passed at precisely that moment. He was a dark, stocky young man, who, oblivious to her presence, glanced casually in through the door. She was standing motionless behind the grille, nonchalant, apparently distracted, a glint of boldness and fear in her restless eyes, following the man as he passed, following the wake left behind by his slow, deliberate, swaying walk, by the sound of his sudden rasping cough. She felt the cold iron beneath her hand and saw the closed door. There was Saturday striding off down the street. She realized that her husband was holding the glass-panelled door open for her to pass. And she turned and calmly, silently followed him, one step at a time; for some reason, she slipped a hand, bewildered and perplexed, into her handbag, as if feeling for something, a key, her powder compact, her handkerchief, that missing piece of Saturday.

THE LETTER

"TODAY I'M GOING TO WRITE to my brother. Do you want to add a note or something?"

"Yes, why not…"

"Or, indeed, why?" he thought. "After all, Luis is my family, not hers."

He was still in his dressing gown, unwashed and uncombed, and was wandering, apparently aimlessly, about the bedroom. Then he went downstairs and hovered indecisively in front of the desk there.

He walked back to the foot of the stairs and shouted:

"Geny, have you got the letter?"

"What letter?"

"The last one Luis wrote to me."

"No, you must have put it somewhere. I've no idea where it is."

He returned to the desk, riffled through a few bits of paper and envelopes, before realizing that he couldn't really see. He felt in his pockets and went back to the foot of the stairs.

"Geny…"

"What?"

"Throw my glasses down to me, will you? I think I left them on the chair in the bedroom, on top of the newspaper."

She took quite a while to reappear, and he thought: "God, she's slow. All she has to do is look where I told her to look. But, then, one of her great pleasures in life is not finding what she's looking for."

"Are you there?" asked his wife from the top of the stairs.

"Where do you think I am?"

"Here, catch."

And she threw him a metal glasses case.

He returned to the desk and rummaged through papers, Christmas cards, leaflets, bills and a few letters.

"Oh, what does it matter?" he thought. "There's no earthly reason why I should remember what Luis said in his letter. It's months since he wrote it. I can tell him about us and ask how his grandson is doing. He'll like that."

He sat down in the armchair opposite the blank television and heard Geny moving about in the kitchen, possibly having breakfast. He shouted:

"Geny, what's Luis's grandson called? Lucas?"

There was the sound of water filling the sink and the clatter of pots and pans. He got up, opened the kitchen door and asked the question again. Geny said:

"Wherever did you get the name 'Lucas' from? No one in either of our families is called Lucas. It's Martín. They called him Martín because he was born on St Martin's Day, the eleventh of November, and they liked the name, don't you remember?"

He went back to his armchair and thought: "They never fail. When it comes to births, saints' days, weddings, divorces and deaths, they're infallible. But that's women for you."

He said to himself: "I could tell Luis that our daughter came and spent a few days with us at Christmas or I could even"—and he smiled at this—"tell him about this morning, when I woke up and saw Geny sitting on the edge of the bed. I suddenly noticed the flowers on her nightdress. I'd never noticed them before. I thought: 'Why flowers?' I never will understand this grotesque desire of Geny's, and of all women, to wear something pretty when all prettiness is fast fading. When you've lived with someone for years, there's no room for lies, there's no way you can disguise or brighten the passing days with a touch of make-up or a nice floral print. I said to her: 'Are you getting up, then, you and your flowers?' I don't know if she heard me or not. She left the room—limping because of her arthritis—and didn't say a word."

"Are you going to have your breakfast now? Are you getting dressed?"

"No, I'm going to write that letter," he said.

Then, feeling a bit chilly, he decided that he would, after all, get washed and dressed.

When he came downstairs again, carrying the notepaper and an envelope, Geny was just finishing preparing some greens and a bit of meat for lunch and told him not to sit at the kitchen table. He picked up a banana and went into the dining room to write.

"Are you going to eat that now?"

"It's my breakfast."

He sat for a moment, looking at the blank sheet, then launched in with: "Dear Luis and Paula". Then he thought: "I don't particularly care about Paula, so I could just write 'Dear Luis' and mention Paula and the children at the end when I send our love to everyone. Or should I start the other way round? 'Dear Paula and Luis', in accordance with that old-fashioned and now defunct rule 'ladies first', or because, in marriages, it's more important to keep in with the wife than with the husband."

"Shall we have lunch?"

"What, now?"

"It's not exactly early. It's gone three o'clock."

He glanced out of the window and it seemed to him that there was less light. It was one of those grey days that gets rapidly greyer and greyer.

When they were having their dessert of stewed apples, she said:

"Loreto said she'd drop by this evening for you to sign a certificate of good character or unimpeachable conduct or some kind of statement saying that we've known them for years…"

"What for?"

"I don't know. I think Piero wants to start a business importing ceramics from Sicily or from Murano or somewhere, and now, what with drug-trafficking and so on, it's not that easy…"

He said nothing and thought about his letter.

After lunch, he fell asleep in the armchair and was woken by Loreto ringing the bell. Geny opened the door, and the two women stood for a while in the hall, whispering.

Loreto was a pretty, dark, plump woman and, when she came in, she filled the apartment with her body, as well as with her voice, her stories, her striking, totem-like eyes, and her laughter. She always wore black to disguise her size—without success.

He liked Loreto and, at the same time, her vitality wore him out, and he preferred to have nothing to do with her husband; he just didn't like him, quite why he didn't know, but, still, they were good neighbours, and so he signed the form.

The letter was still there on the dining table when she left, and he sat down again, intending to carry on.

"Dear Luis and Paula," he read.

"The fact is," he thought, "Luis is the more active of the two of us and could at least phone occasionally, like Geny's sister-in-law does. With letters you never know if they've arrived or not and months or even a year can pass before they're answered, and, besides, I don't really know what to say, because that business about Geny's nightdress would be fine in a diary or your memoirs, but really the only thing you want when you write to someone is to find out if they're all right and to tell them that you, thank God, are also all right."

He wrote: "Your letter reached us ages ago, and this morning I said to Geny that today was the day, that I was going to write and tell you that we're all fine here, with nothing much to report, just the usual aches and pains that come with old age and which, when all's said and done, are at least a sign that we're still alive. Let us know how little Martín is, if he's grown a lot and what tricks he gets up to."

Geny interrupted him because there was a programme about the Normandy landings on Channel 2.

"When?"

"Any minute now."

They watched it together, while she busied herself with some knitting for the Hospital for Children with Spina Bifida. He fell asleep towards the end, before the Führer took personal command. When he woke, they ate some cheese and biscuits and some fruit and, after watching the nine o'clock news, slowly got ready for bed.

"Did you write the letter?"

"No. When did I have time?"

He lay down on his side, thinking about what he had written and noticed that Geny had got into bed wearing her floral-print nightdress. And, still looking at those flowers, he gradually drifted off to sleep.

NALA AND DAMAYANTI

NALA LIVED on his country estate, and the cat, the dog, the horse, the housemaid, the scullery maid, the old cook, the estate manager, the day labourer and anyone else who happened to pass by all gazed at him. Nala was like a god.

Damayanti lived on her country estate, neither very near nor very far from Nala, and when she passed, the flowers opened, the stream leapt, the birds sang, the clouds vanished, the oak tree bowed low, the old ash tree clamoured murmurously and the ilex simpered coyly like a procuress from long, long ago. Damayanti was like a goddess.

One day, beside the battered old car abandoned by the hen house, Nala found a brightly coloured football. It could have belonged to his younger brother Puskara, except that he had never played football. Nala kicked the ball as hard as he could and sent it soaring up into the sky, where it disappeared from sight.

Damayanti was splashing and jumping about in the pool with her girlfriends when she heard a dull plop. A coloured ball spun and glittered on the surface of the water. Damayanti swam gaily over to pick it up, but the ball slipped majestically away along one of the overflow channels. She climbed out of the water and ran after the ball. She picked it up and studied it carefully. The ball showed evident signs of fatigue; it was breathing wearily through its one lung. After a while, Damayanti heard a voice telling her: "The one who sent me has flexible muscles, is tireless, powerful and young."

That evening, Damayanti consulted the oldest people on the estate about wind direction and distances, and found out where the ball had come from.

Shortly afterwards, her father, Bhima, threw a lavish party.

People came from all over, even the three famous and incalculably wealthy landowners called Indra, Agni and Kali. Then, from outside the iron gates, came a long, victorious blast from Nala's car horn, and when he entered, there issued forth from the mouths of all the women an irrepressible murmur of pleasure. Music was playing. Couples were dancing. Nala and Damayanti slowly surrendered their red hearts, which—now partnered, now alone—were galloping ever faster and rapidly ripening and swaying on the warm branch of the dance.

Indra, Agni and Kali were outraged. They stared insolently at Damayanti. They took it in turns to speak to her. They brandished the glittering gold of their words, looks, teeth, pockets, jewels, buttons, fingers, ears, noses, buttonholes. Damayanti hesitated. What would her kind father say when he learnt that she had rejected the landowners' fortunes? But it seemed to her that these gentlemen, like gods laden with ex-votos, lacked substance; they flitted back and forth, their feet not even touching the ground, and their handsome, well-bred eyes, apparently made to gaze upon great things, were hard and inexpressive and still, like plump little glasses filled with liqueur. Damayanti's heart settled on the young man who was tossing a ball over the warm heads of the other girls, a ball presaging vigour and strength. She settled on Nala.

And so they married. And they lived on his country estate. And they were happy. And they had a son and a daughter.

But Nala was mad about playing poker dice. He never just bought a Martini. He either lost it or won it.

And so the landowner Kali, who could not forgive the happy couple, made a pact with Puskara, who was never gazed at by the cat, the dog, the horse, the bull, the housemaid, the scullery maid, the old cook, the day labourer or the estate manager. Who was never gazed at by anyone.

He said to Puskara: "Play dice with your brother day and night. All the gold I have glitters at your back. We will ruin him. His good luck will never be such as to reach the very bottom of our purses. Our luck, on the other hand, will sweep away his entire fortune."

And day by day, Nala, bent over the card table and blind to the consequences, lost his wedding ring, his watch, his tiepin, his diamond cufflinks, his Alfa Romeo, his Mercedes 180, his Ferrari—with its wild, fast engine— his clothes, his lands, his house and even the gaze of those who never tired of gazing at him.

Damayanti wept. What else could she do? And one evening, when the first lights were being lit, she secretly took her two children and left them at her father's house.

"Now all you have left is Damayanti," Puskara said to Nala. Meanwhile, Kali, intoxicated, overjoyed and fully avenged, was watching in triumph, with one piercing eye pressed to the keyhole.

When Nala heard his wife's name, he stood up. Fearfully, like the child who steals the milk intended for an invalid, like the blind man in a world ablaze with light, and filled with the bitter solitude of all great libertines and all great sages, he made his way to Damayanti's bedroom.

He said nothing. He entered the room in silence, his face as white as the sheets that covered him as he slipped into bed; with a strange light in his eyes, he stroked his wife's soft hair, her hands and shoulders.

At midnight, when Damayanti was sleeping, he got up and left the house for ever.

He wrote her only a few parting words: "Now that I am about to lose you, my love grows ever stronger. I cannot taint your life with my misfortune. The bed that, tonight, gave shelter to our uneasy sleep is no longer ours. Nothing in this house belongs to us. But one day, I will be worthy of you. I promise. I will remake the fortune I have lost and seek you out day and night in order to pay you in kisses for each tear you have shed."

Given that the forests of the world lie too far off, Damayanti did not plunge into them to weep over his misfortune. We men may have travelled to the moon, but we never know anything about what happens in the Earth's forests, and had this story not occurred near the city and affected two respectable families, no one would ever have known anything about it.

Damayanti did not want to move back into her father's house, and so she set off into the world in search of Nala. She worked as a lady's companion, a research assistant, an English teacher, an interpreter in a fashion house, the manageress of a hotel, a window dresser.

Nala sought his fortune by every available route. He was a docker, a car salesman, a barman, a chauffeur, a taxi driver, an opening act for big-name stars.

Damayanti's father, Bhima, immediately summoned Sudeva—a shrewd, veteran police inspector, working now as a private detective—and engaged him on a full-time basis, his mission being to find both Nala and Damayanti.

Inspector Sudeva fell asleep in his seat, legs crossed, on innumerable trains; he arrived in strange cities; he spent whole mornings and afternoons in districts full of market stalls; he ate hundreds of sandwiches in cinemas with continuous showings; he had his eyes tested and bought new glasses; from the windows of old cafés, he watched people of all classes and at all hours of the day; in every park, he threw children their ball and he waited, yawning, in every doorway, for the rain to ease.

Sudeva knew perfectly well that Damayanti was working as a hat-check girl in a club. The first time he saw her, he watched her until late at night. At ten o'clock, a man appeared—young, slim, tall, dark and wearing a blue overcoat—and took her dancing. At dawn, the couple disappeared into a hotel.

This is what Damayanti was thinking about that dark young man called Maisure: "Sometimes he does things that Nala might have done."

A year and a half later, Sudeva saw her again. This time she was with an equally young man, although this time he was pink-skinned and fair and muscular. Standing on a street corner, they were exchanging a very long, awkward kiss.

Damayanti was thinking about the fair-haired man: "He often reminds me of Nala and also, a little, of Maisure."

Sudeva also knew that Nala was currently working

118

for an advertising agency. Just as he was despairing of ever finding him, he spotted him drinking a dry Martini with a kind of young Damayanti. She was dark, slender, and with a smile that Sudeva took great pains to study. The inspector deduced or, rather, intuited that there was more to this affair than mere words.

Nala was thinking about Shimoga, the dark young woman: "Sometimes she does what Damayanti used to do."

A while later, Sudeva saw him again walking by a river, under an umbrella, arm in arm with a svelte, red-haired woman with nice legs. The couple sat down beneath the arch of the bridge, while Sudeva, up above, was thinking his own thoughts as he gazed down at the river.

It seemed to Nala that the woman was sometimes like Damayanti and sometimes like Shimoga.

Sudeva was old now. His job allowed him to live very comfortably. He looked for Nala and Damayanti, but always took special care never to find them. He had thought deeply about this. He would not allow the story to end well, because he didn't want it to end badly. Things are as they are, and not even a father can change them. Besides, it was so pleasant to be eternally employed by a gentleman: a fine, rich, kind-hearted gentleman like the magnanimous Bhima!

REPARATION

For José Luis Castillo Puche,
with thanks for the loan of these two characters

T HEY TOOK JUANA to the cemetery. The funeral was
attended by a number of old people of Frasquito's
age, by Juana's brother-in-law, their nephews and three
or four women. Juana and Frasquito were well-known
figures locally. Originally because, though poor themselves, they were distant relatives of Don Roque, the
richest man in the village. Later, they became famous
because four years earlier they had been the victims of a
robbery. When Don Roque died, he left them a vineyard
in the neighbouring village. Since they had no children,
they sold the vineyard. And afterwards, on the train back,
all the money from the sale was stolen from them, and
with it the prospect of a comfortable old age and a trip to
Valencia to get Juana's teeth fixed. The civil guard never
found out who was responsible. Originally, Juana and
Frasquito were referred to as "Don Roque's relatives".
Later, they were known as "the couple who got robbed".

Juana's death—which was hastened by the distress caused by the robbery and by the civil war—had prompted people to start gossiping again about that famous incident. And as Frasquito walked behind the coffin, he caught the odd word, snatches of conversation, comments and even the occasional muffled laugh, doubtless alluding to the robbery on the train. Not even three years of civil war had erased the memory of that event. A feeling of helpless rage began to take hold of Frasquito, and as he threw the first handful of earth onto the coffin, he muttered darkly, his words muffled by sobs: "They're going to give it all back, Juana. You'll see. All of it." None of those present knew what he meant, and they listened, eyes fixed coldly and respectfully on the ground, believing that they had heard a promise, an oath or the announcement of something that time would take it upon itself to crumple and cast to the winds.

The people attending the funeral lined up to shake the hand of the widower, Juana's brother-in-law and the nephews, and then they formed into groups or couples as they strolled back to the village, rolling cigarettes, chatting about the state of the fields and turning their backs on that alien death.

That night, Frasquito chose not to stay with any of his nephews. He managed to endure until quite late in the day the company of his family and those three or four women who had arranged for them all to pray the rosary. Then he went back alone to the house where he had always lived with Juana. He bolted the door, placed a straw mattress and a blanket behind it, and there, with his feet almost touching the door of their bedroom, he lay very still in the darkness, staring up at the ceiling, thinking about what death must be like and wondering whether his Juana would be feeling terribly alone and cold and perhaps filled with dumb, inexpressible grief to find he was no longer at her side, as he always had been, with the sudden realization that he had left her there, far beneath the earth, as if she, poor, innocent, childlike Juana, would be capable of understanding a death as serious, irreparable and permanent as that. "Juana, my love, you must get used to not being with me, just for a while at first, and then awhile longer, and then a bit more. The earth is dry and hard and blind, but the Lord God understands, my dear, and, gradually, with a slow, firm hand, He will change you so that you no longer turn to look at me, so that you can bear to spend whole days without me"—here his eyes filled with tears—"and it may even be better for you, you might even be happier, and one day, Juana, you will learn how the people who robbed us are suffering down in hell."

No. He was sure that the very obliging man from the train was still alive. Had he been the thief? Or was it the photographer with the horse, who had taken their picture in the village square? He didn't know. He had never known. It had been all of them. The brusque, starchy notary who had rushed them through the sale; the Gómez brothers, who, when they bought the vineyard, had rolled their eyes and laughed, all the while insisting that they had given them a good price; the mediator Carrasco; the men standing in the square in their long, dark smocks, eyeing them insolently, mischievously, mockingly; the sacristan in the church, which Juana had insisted on entering in order to pay for a mass for Don Roque; the packed train itself, full of people, loud voices, smoke, sun and wind, full of inexplicable, lurching stops and starts, of comings and goings and vehement pushings and shovings. It had all been a rascally plot to relegate them once more to the miserly wage they could earn from working the land, to their previous state of desolate, domestic poverty. But he didn't care any more. Raising his eyebrows and looking back at the cemetery, he murmured: "I may not be here to tend the dead, Juana, but just remember: they're going to pay back all the money they stole from us, right down to the last peseta. Perhaps God will arrange for the wind to send you the occasional flower." Then, when the light seeping in through the cracks in the yard door took on a bluish tinge, he got up in silence and stood hesitating for a while outside their bedroom. In the end, he pushed the door open and went in, determined that he would look at nothing, that he would barely breathe. On a chair, he saw his corduroy suit. He put it on hurriedly, clumsily.

He opened the bottom drawer of the potbellied dresser, and a pair of dark, bright, peasant eyes looked up at him from a piece of card. There they were in their wedding photo, stiff and as if rooted to the spot, but she was the person you immediately noticed, not him. He put the photo away in his inside jacket pocket. He picked up a grey sweater, a blanket, his black scarf and his black cap. Then he stumbled, almost choking, from the room and stood leaning against the wall in the corridor, two tears running down his cheeks, because, despite himself, he had felt Juana's presence, smelt her; her human warmth was still there in the bedroom. She smelt as he knew Juana always did on a Sunday. And the dresser was full of her. As the darkness outside was beginning to swell with light, he opened the door, as alone now as he had been on the cruelly bright, fateful day when he had last stepped out of the house with Juana and walked slowly to the station, where he sat down and waited. The train hove into view like a vast, grubby shadow, like a great black panting beast forced by its driver to slice a path through the dawn light. He got out his ticket. He climbed into the carriage. When the train drew out of the station, the fields looked numb with cold, the wind was whistling and there were still stars in the sky. "Such a bitter night! How hard it must be for the newly dead! Poor Juana, abandoned to the darkness! What a horrible thing it is to shovel earth onto a life, as if to do so were a mere ritual, almost a

game, and never to raise that life up again. Never!"
Frasquito was staring, wide-eyed, out of the window
and moving cracked, trembling lips: "Goodbye, Juana!
Goodbye, Juana, my love!" The platform was empty.
He waved at the flagstones, waving goodbye to his dead
wife, who had also been like an inseparable sister to him.
He looked at the village roofs, the school, Don Roque's
house, the church, the town-hall tower, and, at the first
bend, he caught sight of the west wall of the cemetery
and a cypress tree. There she was, with no alternative
now but to accustom herself to death, slowly letting go
of Frasquito's warm kisses, of the female, physical web
of household chores, the chatter and laughter with the
next-door neighbour, the long, warm, delicious evenings
sitting by the front door—all cold now, all gone. There she
was, sadly, opaquely, entering a world so large, so formal,
so landless that in it she would be nothing. And yet poor
Juana, who had been made for this lowly, humble world,
was now incredibly important, for she was entering the
unstoppable, meandering river of eternity.

When he got off the train, the morning was bright and
warm, glazed with sunlight. Juana, he thought, would
now be recovering from that first horrible, cold, lonely
night, stretching drowsily and aware perhaps of a bird
singing and a faint glimmer of light from above. Frasquito
walked slowly down the streets, which smelt slightly of
aniseed, clay water pitchers and esparto grass. The large,

scruffy, luminous village where the robbery had taken place was still waking up. When he reached the square, he looked dully this way and that, then sat down on a bench. There were men standing around talking or in silence, just as there had been when he and Juana came to sell their inheritance. A few little girls passed, carrying water. A man with a donkey went by, crying his wares. And an ancient black Ford, covered in mud and dust, was urgently, loudly sounding its horn, as, with some difficulty, it made its way through the waiting crowd of men. On a corner, underneath the arches, was a notice proclaiming: Notary. That where it had all begun. Perhaps they had been followed when they left the office. Someone in the know might have warned some heartless person or persons. With a shiver, Frasquito thought of Juana and clutched the handle of his crook, his body stiffening and his eyes filling with tears. He had come here to beg for alms, to beg back what was his by rights, peseta by peseta, and to live on what he begged from these people until the end. They would give back every peseta. Yes, he would live on what was owed to him until he died. He neither could nor wished to work any more. He had kept working as long as Juana was alive, because she would never have allowed him to become a beggar. Nor did he ever reveal his intentions to her, because she would have made him swear never to do it. He had it all planned out, though. What one person robs another person begs. Wherever there are thieves there must be beggars. He imagined their money scattered among the families in the village, forming, as it spread, a network of ditches, a family tree of that infamous act. Almost everyone would have some small change from that robbery in their waistcoat pocket. Now, though, they would all pay their dues.

He went over to the church. There were two beggars sitting on the ground by the door, and Frasquito raised a hand in greeting. Then he kept his eyes fixed on them as if to say: "There's no way you're going to shift me from here." At first, the beggars stared down at the ground, then averted their gaze entirely as if dazzled by the sun. He sat on the steps, placed his black cap upside down beside him and waited, all the time moving his lips as he had seen the other beggars do whenever anyone passed by. A few women went in and out of the church. Coins began to gleam dully against the black fabric of his cap, began to fall like sparse, plump raindrops. He sat very still, gazing at the distant fields beyond the streets. They weren't giving him charity, but justice. They were unhurriedly, coin by coin, paying back what they allowed him. Charity would be his monetary salvation. He was free to think his own thoughts, while they were convinced they were buying themselves a place in the next world.

When midday came, the other beggars left, and the sun alone crept slowly up the church steps—a hot, golden sun. From an alleyway came the asthmatic smell of oil and fried fish. Frasquito did not yet have enough money to buy any food and so he waited patiently, filled by a certain perverse delight. He was waiting for the novena and for evening confession. Having nothing else to do, he slipped timidly into the church, and on the nearest flagstone, next to the door and the holy water stoup, he offered up a prayer for Juana to God, who was there at the far end of the church, bristling with gold. He realized that he was at liberty to do this every day and felt beatifically happy.

Frasquito gradually became accepted as a bona fide recipient of public charity, a customary sight for almoners, the perfect beggar. His clothes grew more suited to his condition with each day that passed, became worn, dusty, meek. Frasquito slept in rocky shelters, pressed close to the walls against the cold. He lined up at the doors of the barracks or the convent with his shiny broad tin dish. People often tried to throw him out because he wasn't from the village. However, he knew that those who have enough to eat and dislike getting their hands dirty always tire long before those who have little to eat and are accustomed to dirtying their hands, and so all their attempts at ejection failed. Now and then he would talk out loud. He was with Juana then. At other times, at night, he would lie close to the earth so that she could hear his voice more clearly. Juana had already experienced the fiery sun on her grave, the heavy, icy rain that pitilessly pierces and drenches the dead, the anchor of death about their neck. Juana was definitively, inexorably dead.

He spent almost every night doing his sums. "They've already given us back eight thousand two hundred pesetas, eight thousand three hundred pesetas, eight thousand three hundred and ninety-seven pesetas." He was counting for Juana's benefit, although he had already forgotten many things about her and would spend whole weeks stubbornly trying to remember them, sometimes without success. Juana was becoming just a name, an incorporeal companion, a vague figure who was still, for some reason, mysteriously bound to him. He lived like this for six years, and then one night, weary and white with frost, his heart stopped. In his jacket pocket they found the faded, greasy wedding photo folded in two. And two grubby sheets of paper covered in pencilled scribblings. One sheet was full of sums, with one amount overwritten and underlined several times. And on the other sheet were the words: "Bury me with Juana in Hécula. My name is Frasquito."

That man had cost the village 42,318 pesetas. According to his calculations, justice still owed charity 82,677 pesetas—more or less.

FULL STOP

D ON ELOY MILLÁN walked into the classroom. It had felt rather cool out in the corridor and, as he went in, a warm incubator smell wrapped about him. It was a sweet, soft blend of pencils, stale, innocent pee and dried soap behind young ears. The boys got to their feet. Don Eloy Millán went straight to his desk without looking at them.

"Good morning, Don Eloy."

"Good morning, Señor Millán."

The class was split like that every day. Some called him Señor Millán, others Don Eloy.

"Right, let's get down to business. Please be seated!"

He always felt awkward saying that, rather than simply "Sit down", but he wanted to instil in them both good grammar and good manners. While in the classroom, he must be a stickler for the rules and thus avoid confusing the children. He must be a shining light to them, at least for that hour. When he spoke, his most important duty was to be an exemplar of grammar and politeness, a steadfast, infallible chronometer.

The boys sat down. Then two of them approached his desk. Every day, at least one boy was sure to come up, although generally for no good reason. One impassively, dumbly held out an open exercise book. Don Eloy looked at him. Then he remembered. During the last class, he had said to the boy: "Tomorrow, bring me your exercise book."

"Silence!" he said, fixing them all with a stern gaze.

Good, the boy had done his homework. Don Eloy took out his mark book and wrote something next to the boy's name.

"All right, go back to your desk… And what do *you* want?"

The other boy waiting approached cautiously. He was very polite, in a fresh, spontaneous, joyous way. He said confidentially, almost brushing Don Eloy's ear with his mouth:

"Good morning, Don Eloy."

"I see," Don Eloy thought, "a personal greeting. Very nice." Then he said: "Today is Friday and therefore dictation day. You should have your workbooks ready on your desks."

He heard the rustle of pages being turned. Frowning, he searched meticulously through the contents of his briefcase. No, the "Pedagogical dictation texts" were not there. He had left them at home. He pondered what to do. He pushed out his lips and gnawed the inside of his lower lip. What could he use as a text?

"Silence!" he said, raising his voice, when he heard the inevitable rising wave of murmuring. "I'm just trying to find…"

He had all kinds of bits of paper in his briefcase. The fourth-year book wouldn't be any use for this class. There was an old newspaper. "No, definitely not the newspaper," he said resolutely, as if guarding the children from something bad. Suddenly he remembered. There was a letter he had spent several days over. He had typed out a few versions, all slightly different. He was really pleased with the way certain paragraphs had turned out. Yes, why not? Azorín, Pereda, Bécquer, Leandro Fernández de Moratín, Juan Ramón Jiménez, Palacio Valdés, Benavente, Rubén Darío, Perrault, Pérez Galdós… And Eloy Millán. Yes, why not? After all, some years back, he'd had a number of articles published in his home town, which, at the time, already had a population of more than eighty thousand. Yes, why not? He would simply dictate part of his letter, and the boys would assume that it was some special test, created expressly for them, perhaps drawn from a book, or invented, a "lie" taken from some literary text.

"Right, Martínez Lago, come to the front, will you? As usual, you will write what I dictate on the blackboard. The rest of you, without looking up, must write what I dictate in your workbooks. I don't want to see anyone looking at the blackboard. Just concentrate on your own work."

He leafed through the various versions of the letter, looking for an appropriate paragraph.

"What's the title?" asked one boy.

Don Eloy hesitated.

"No title. Just 'Dictation'. Let's begin."

"Wait!" cried a shrill, anguished voice.

"What's wrong now?"

"Nothing, sir. It's just that I can't find my pen. Can I do it in pencil?"

"Right, I'm going to start now."

He stood up. He glanced out of the window and then, in a slow, clear, sonorous voice, he dictated the following paragraph:

"Things are not the same now. Behind those poplars one used to be able to see the cathedral tower, the besieging swifts at evening and, beyond that, the mountains and the pure colours of the fields, picked out by the sun. If I could choose a tree in which to be as happy as the birds, you know very well that I would choose a poplar. Even if it was the one I can see from my window, in the doomed garden, on the building plot that will soon be filled with bricks. They offered us a fringe of shade each afternoon, and the constant chatter of their leaves made you say those words I did not dare to think about until much later. Until only recently. Do you remember? I wonder."

"Full stop."

The class stirred. Some boys huffed and puffed, flexed their wrist or furiously shook their supposedly weary right hand. They did this whenever the dictation lasted even a little longer than usual. They were playing at "overwork", at "exhaustion".

"All right, let's check for any mistakes."

Martínez Lago had spelt "poplars" with "er" not "ar", reversed the "i" and the "e" in "besieging" and left out "fringe" altogether.

"And no elision of 'I would…'"

Don Eloy read out the phrase with particular emphasis: "You know very well that I would choose a poplar…"

He remained sunk in thought for a moment. His heart, pointlessly, kept time: tick-tock, tick-tock…

"Sir! Sir!" came a small, insistent voice from the back row. "This boy says you can have a capital letter after a comma."

"As I was saying, in prose there should be no elision of 'I would'. All right, go and sit down again."

Don Eloy Millán also sat down. A hearty, anonymous hubbub began to fill the classroom. Don Eloy looked up at the window. The sad, towering mass of clouds grew darker in the distance. An ashen light cast shifting, bruising shadows on things, threatening to impose a Messianic law of boredom and loneliness, of damp, defenceless, endless hours, thunderous and monotonous, a melancholy frame to the day-to-day tasks. A day of light bulbs prematurely lit, a day when the entrance hall would fill up with anxious mothers, with prattle and umbrellas and raincoats. A day like a vast, inexplicable cloud of smoke that left the eyes red with solitude.

"Have you finished correcting your work? All of you?"

"Yes, sir."

"No, not yet. Just a moment. Right!"

"Sir, shall I clean the board?"

"No!"

He felt crushed, invaded. "Lord," he thought, "was there no respite! Why that insatiable need for change and agitation, why the rush? They were always wanting to move on to the next thing, and those now old words on the board stood in their way, words that only a moment before had been unknown to them and even distant and worthy of respect, with their possible lurking orthographical traps. They want to erase them, to erase me, to discard the tender, unctuous, white splendour of those words, to reduce them to dust, to cast them to the winds like so many dead cells hampering their growth, like the steam on a window that obscures their view of the road, like an old horse fallen in the race, and all because of that need to write and get on in life, to erase and write again, to grow and erase and write again and to become men." And where was he in all this? Buried beneath a cold heap of dead verbs, adverbs, adjectives, nouns and prepositions?

"Shall I clean the board?"

"No, I said 'No'."

He was defending his words now like a cornered animal. He called for silence. The boys could already sense that it was time for the end-of-lesson bell to ring. The proximity of that moment made them restless. They kept looking out of the window, at the boys at the back of the class, at the coats hanging on the coat-rack... Don Eloy Millán was a kind man. He was distracted. Perhaps he had a headache or was tired. There was a flash followed by a distant rumble of thunder. The boys glanced up at the clouds for a moment, slightly pale, slightly troubled and excited, as if they were watching the approach of a majestic, silent, deadly caravel. He set them an exercise to do from their books. He asked Cubero where in the exercises they had got to. He walked up and down the centre aisle between the desks. He gazed from the back of the room at his words written on the blackboard, his own words. The clouds were stealing rhythmically, hurriedly away towards other places in the world.

"Sir, shall I clean the board?"

"Can I, Don Eloy?"

The bell rang. The boys sprang to their feet, noisily snatching up their satchels and putting away their books, scraping chairs and desks, taking their coats from the rack and calling to one another. One of them grabbed the board rubber and, tenaciously, from top to bottom, from left to right, with wild, forceful, feline gestures, cleaned the whole blackboard.

Don Eloy Millán slowly picked up his briefcase and his coat from the desk.

"Bye, sir!"

"Goodbye, Don Eloy!"

"Goodbye, Señor Millán! See you tomorrow!"

He was left alone, putting on his gloves. He thought: "They didn't even erase me slowly." He was looking at the black rectangular board, like a precise, deep, dark hole. The now silent blackboard. *He* had been written on that board and now *he* had been erased. And with such rancour, such haste! His heart, he sensed, was clouding over. "How many others like me," he thought, "lie behind that board, forgotten, lost, erased for ever, just like that?"

He stood for a long while, staring at the blackboard, anxiously searching for a fragment of just one of his words or even half a word, anything, the tail of a letter, the dot on an "i", searching for himself, fearfully searching that black rectangle.

THE CAR

I WANT TO PAY HOMAGE to the car because it has borne us on its back for many years now. Don't ask me about the engine, the make, the number plate, what kind of fuel it uses, or even if it was mine, because after looking at it all these years, I no longer know to whom it belonged: to me, to him or to her, or to those who came and went and shared the journey with us for a season or longer.

The car carried us along like a cheerful, trusting blind man. There was a pillow inside, some old blankets, a few guides and maps, breadcrumbs, dried rosemary, a rip in the fabric made by a child, mud from the tracks—long since crumbled to dust—left by a dog from Navas del Rey, who really loved us. There were other things besides, which were hard to explain or at least hard to believe. If I were a teller of tales, the car itself would be speaking by now. But then the car, for me, would be a worthless fool. We were the ones who talked—or didn't talk—while the car behaved like what it was: a car.

The car even took us out at dawn, when we were still half asleep. Past pine trees or oaks, past olive trees. In sun and rain, laughing or sad, like the fields, the streams, the animals and the noises at dusk.

The carpets were not exactly what one would find in a palace, but they had felt the spur of the kind of high heels favoured by young women, and even the occasional lone shoe, possibly lost at midnight, and whose other half I never did find. And briefcases, too, containing notes, poems, books.

We argued violently in the car, as if we could not simply get out and escape from one another, as if it were the only room in the world. We would sing, too, as we used to at school. We made plans as if we were going to stop the car right there and immediately put those plans into action. We occasionally grew irritated when we were driving along without knowing why, and it seemed as if something that had been ours had got mislaid along the way, to the right or to the left, or we felt sure that out there lay another world and other people, too, and we felt distant from each other, prisoners of the car, yes, prisoners. There were times when we needed to fill the car with a different voice, a different hope, a different life. And on days like that, we almost forgot about the car, which was like forgetting about ourselves.

I don't quite know who we were or even if we knew ourselves. I remember her fair hair—simple, natural— and how he, sometimes, had to strain his voice to be heard above the engine noise. On many days, no one saw us pass and we saw no one. Air, rivers, skies, trees. The road was a strange, sleeping, endless blue vein. Had God ordained a new Noah's Ark without us knowing? We also saw a lot of people pass, inside and outside the car. Ah, if that car could only speak...

The car was a waiting room. We waited for grief and also for happiness, or simply to find out if that mysterious thing, the heart, was still beating. On hot days, the car itself seemed to be beating. Perhaps we were waiting to love each other more or to part one day as everyone does.

Sometimes the car was like a distinguished, comfortable, well-cut suit. At others, it was so ill-fitting that we felt awkward in it.

Its engine made no more noise than a Sunday crowd or the fountain in the square or school children reciting their times tables. I can't hear the noise it makes, or perhaps I hear it all the time. It travelled at a human speed, and we were its sole destination. I can hear its silence too.

I could be more precise, but I don't want you then to tell me that the same thing happened to you once or to a friend or relative of yours. Although I know these things do happen. I just want to say that the car bore us away and can't come back; it never has, it has always simply gone, don't ask me where. You, too, have a car? Yes, but that, of course, isn't what I mean... I mean something else...

We rarely ate in it, no; we thought, talked, looked, loved, hated. (Hated? No, I don't think so.) With friends who were only there for a while and with lifelong buddies, with anodyne or occasional acquaintances and even with people wearing cassocks and habits, as if we were on our final journey. An opening and closing of doors farther up the road. A turning on and off of the lights farther up the road. Get out this side... Get in here... Come on... Today we're going to...

As far as I know, this car has never knocked anyone down. Apart from us occasionally. Once, a bird crashed into it—even though we weren't exactly travelling through the highways of the air at the time. The thud of that bird hitting the car was a stone thrown by God and it made us shudder and fall silent and think. In spring and summer, insects splattered the car—squashed, dead, shapeless, still fluttering. That's how it was.

We have been to so many places that a lot of them have been erased as if we had never been there at all. We have seen so many people that we could go back and reintroduce ourselves. What joy and sadness there was in all those exits and entrances! What a shame we couldn't have got into another car or followed the road we passed back there on the right or the left! And what a shame that we must leave this one behind! One day, the car will drive us itself.

Where is it? What's happened to it? Nothing. We're

still here, still in the car. But I looked at it rather differently today, the way you might look at your own arm, with the attachment, disbelief and anxiety with which some of us look at ourselves in the mirror.

SEÑOR OTAOLA, NATURAL SCIENCES

SEÑOR OTAOLA would go up the stairs at nine o'clock sharp, with an absent look in his eyes, a cold, correct expression on his face, and, if he happened to pass a colleague, he would raise one long, pale, bony hand in greeting. When he spoke to someone, he would bend deferentially towards him or her, wrinkling up his whole face in an attempt at a smile, and address them quietly, seriously, in clipped, military tones. Señor Otaola did not get out of breath climbing the stairs. He did not change his pace if something happened nearby. He merely looked very hard at the perpetrator, with cold, condemnatory eyes and a slightly haughty, weary look of deep under-standing. Señor Otaola taught Natural Sciences. There was no haggling over marks with him; each pupil had to accept what he was given and that was that. And the mark stayed there, in the teacher's mark book, waiting to be added up at the end of term. His classes were not noisy or intense, but diverting and gentle.

In winter, at nine o'clock in the morning, the cold in the classroom was as taut as a drum. Señor Otaola, who always wore a waistcoat, never wore an overcoat, raincoat or waterproofs while at school. Perhaps he left them in the staff room or the secretary's office. He began the lesson impassively, as if the cold did not affect him, striding up and down the central aisle between the desks. It was very, very cold, and yet he spoke about silkworms, ladybirds, grasshoppers and butterflies. Those flies, dragonflies and grasshoppers gradually warmed the hearts of the boys, as if it were summer or else spring, late spring: the sun poured in through the windows, the shadows cast by the leaves of a poplar blinked and flickered on the desks; in the Natural Sciences class there really were flies, and then Señor Otaola would speak about sandstone, rushing streams, fluvial erosion, waterfalls, glaciers, moraine, erratic blocks...

Señor Otaola had a hoarse, muffled voice, as if he were suffering the chronic after-effects of some youthful expedition into jungles or up rivers. He would often half close his pale eyes as if the landscape he was describing dazzled him: the bright reflection from the pelagic zone of the sea, the sparse vegetation of the tundra, or the knifelike ridge of a rock. Señor Otaola wore gold cuff-links, a pocket watch and a wedding ring.

At nine o'clock, he went up the stairs to take his class, sometimes teaching one year, sometimes another. At ten o'clock he came down. He could be seen smoking a cigarette and pacing about in the entrance hall, and when there was a school meeting, he would punctually take his place, silent, but never hermetically so. He would greet the mothers of the children, the female teachers and the cleaners with a gesture that was parsimonious, yet gentlemanly and fulsome. In his classes all was peace and respect, the respect imposed by his measured words, his affable remoteness, his tone of voice, his conscientiousness, the exemplary irrevocability of everything he did in the classroom. Señor Otaola's classes, his every step, were as they were, and nothing could change them. Knowing him, one could understand why the heavenly spheres do not bump into each other, why Nature always arrives promptly each spring, bearing flowers, why it never forgets the formula for making clouds, why life and death reach into so many corners in wise, miraculous silence. Glaciers in spring, blossoms in winter. And his slow hands moving in the air, dissecting imagined hexapods, ruthlessly stripping the petals from the sterile daisy of science. Did anyone have anything more to add about Señor Otaola?

Only Gil Fajardo in 2C—and it was surely a lie. He said that, over a period of two or three days, right in the middle of a lesson, he had heard the metallic rattle of a cricket. It wasn't the complete sound, he said, more like a gentle strumming, as if the cricket were timidly tuning up its elytra. As if it were agreeing, from its position of animal inferiority, with something Señor Otaola had said about orthoptera or possibly about some other subject, he couldn't quite remember: cryptogams, phanerogams, dunes, the courses of rivers, estuaries, meanders, sandbanks, volcanoes or hydrostatic levels… And, of course, he didn't know whether the sound of the cricket was pretend or real, although it seemed to come from near where Señor Otaola was standing. But that is what Gil Fajardo said later. Before—if it's true what he said—he had kept quiet about it or not believed it. Because he said this after the accident, which was really something rather more than what we would normally describe as an accident.

Señor Otaola had finished his lesson with the third years with his accustomed air of normality. The bell rang to announce the hour. It was ten o'clock. He went down the stairs as usual. And when he had gone down the first flight and was standing on the second landing, he stood looking at the steps before him, twelve of them, and suddenly took a leap, a leap intended to carry him from one landing to the next. Señor Otaola performed this leap with unwonted, childlike glee, although one could also say that he did not entirely lose his air of seriousness. He fell on the seventh stair and rolled down the last five. Señor Otaola broke a leg and sustained injuries to his head and one arm.

The leap was witnessed by Señor Rodríguez, the maths teacher, who was also going down the stairs at that moment, by Señorita Eulalia, the art teacher, who was coming up, and by several pupils from various years, who were racing down the stairs to answer a call of nature.

THE SEA

W E ENDED UP renting an apartment on the Costa Templada, near Almuñécar, one of the areas being promoted by the tourist board at the time.

She was happy. And I wasn't in a bad mood exactly, just a little grumpy.

It turned out that the apartment was new, and there were still spots of paint on the door handles and on the skirting board. The first thing we did was to go into the village and buy cloths, scrubbing brushes, detergent and a litre of turps.

There was nowhere to hang our clothes and, instead of telling the concierge or writing a letter to the owner, I bought some metal hooks and screwed them into the back of the doors in the bedroom and bathroom.

Seeing my wife labouring away removing paint stains, I decided to give her a hand, and for three or four days—of the fifteen days we were going to spend there—I didn't even have time to pick up a book or a pen. When we arrived, I was reading Charles Bally and all that fascinating stuff about the substantivation of the adjective.

I found the turps such a miraculous substance that I opened my suitcase and looked the word up in the dictionary. It turned out to be essence of turpentine, a semi-fluid resin exuded by pines, firs, larches and terebinths. I associated the last with healthy, summer things, which pleased me.

Almost every day we found something else wrong; the bedside table and the chairs were as wobbly as if they had a leg missing, but the sea was so close—we could see it from our balcony—and we went to the sea from day two on.

To get to the sea we had to pass a supermarket and a campsite run by a Belgian. Then we just had to go up a dusty hill, down another one and there we were—at about a quarter past one—at the beach, where one could immediately make out three distinct lines: the shifting line of the water, the dark line of wet sand, and the line formed by the sunshades and awnings with people underneath and around them, and, whether sitting or lying down, all were looking at the sea.

The sun appeared to cause smoke to rise from every surface, and, when I took off my sandals, I had to scamper onto a patch of sand in the shade so as not to burn my feet. My wife, being less sensitive, tougher or more indifferent, followed me.

From her bag she produced a large tube of Nivea—a yellowish cream, especially made to protect you from sunburn—and began rubbing it on my back. The touch of her fingers made me feel numb and tired; I yawned and began to grow bored.

Then she said:

"Would you mind putting some Nivea on my back too?"

I did so, yawning.

There were two classes of humanity on the beach: the bronzed, oily, sweaty variety, and the more refined, reserved sort, who sat in the bluish shade and seemed, oddly, to rule over everyone else.

The sea did not so much murmur as boom, drowning out human voices.

While I was applying Nivea to Merche's back, a fierce, blueblack horsefly appeared, with all guns blazing, determined to bite me. I had the devil's own job shooing it off, because it was as fast and incisive as a cutting remark.

Some yards away a small, fit-looking man was speaking French to two young women lying on the sand; every now and then, he would whistle 'Strangers in the Night' or sing it in English.

The night, of course, any night, bore no resemblance to that overwhelming midday heat that weighed on the shoulders and seemed to rise, burning, from your feet up. Or perhaps it did, perhaps the sun was also a kind of night, which enervated and blinded us, and made us all into strangers "exchanging glances" and "wandering in the night", as the Frenchman kept insisting.

I raised my arms and felt as if I were deflating with weariness.

I went for a short run, and the pebbles cut into my feet. And then, as I walked back, I felt an unpleasant tension in my groin.

Then we went for a swim. Merche plunged straight in, while I thought about it for a while. The water struck cold at first, and once you were in, it never became what you might call warm, as the name Costa Templada suggested it would. We swam for a while; we smiled at each other. We looked and were looked at, blatantly and with impunity, by other heads bobbing about in the water.

Merche said:

"It's lovely, isn't it?"

I didn't answer.

I came out of the water before she did and went for another run, less painful this time, along the wet sand.

Merche stayed in the water as if she had no intention of ever coming out, and I sat down in line with the other humans looking at the sea.

The sea was both relevant and irrelevant, and yet it was the most important thing there. I wouldn't have bothered contemplating the human line or the kiosk with its back to the sea, selling "soft drinks, beverages and sandwiches", nor, farther off, the hills, sticky with heat haze.

No, I had to look at the sea, and not because Merche was still in there, swimming, but because we were all of us drunkards, hypnotized by the sea, because it moved and spoke and was vast.

I sat for a long time, staring at the waves, which were never the same, a fact that filled me with mistrust and unease. People talk about the sea being monotonous, as they do about anything they don't observe closely enough.

The waves were never the same, although they may have repeated themselves in similar cycles. The meaning of the wave never went beyond being a rather comforting mystical murmur. But the sea seemed to express itself in ways superior to the wave, in whole unintelligible paragraphs and speeches, as rich in modes and forms as it was in depths and fishes. On the other hand, I understood nothing of what it said.

I realized that, had I managed to understand, I might have applauded; everyone sitting there staring at the sea might have applauded too; those of us, whether standing or lying down and staring at the sea, were waiting only for a grandiose phrase or an acceptable cliché to spring to our feet and applaud.

By the time Merche emerged from the water, I was feeling almost feverish.

When she had dried herself, we set off back to the apartment.

I asked Merche:

"Do you not think that all this is somehow an idea from God?"

"I don't know. Isn't everything?" she said.

"Yes, of course, but this… It's as if God were trying to tell us something, tell us his idea. Do you understand? There's the sea pounding away, and all that sun and the beach, all totally sterile. And all those naked people. It must be symbolic, don't you think?"

"Symbolic? How should I know!"

"There's something very odd about it all. I can't believe that it's just there for no other reason than for us to come here and fool around. It seems too much fuss for so little. All we really need is a pool or a pulley and some weights. I just don't get it."

"There's nothing *to* get."

"Of course there is. It's trying to put across an idea, a big idea. It's trying to tell us something in an extraordinary language of which I don't understand a word. Not a single word. But never mind, I was ready to leave anyway."

We dropped in at the supermarket, and Merche bought a lovely fresh lettuce, some olives, a beautiful tomato and a tin of tuna.

At night, we sat on the balcony, looking at the sea. We occasionally glanced at the mountains, the road and the other houses on the estate, almost all of them occupied by

153

French and Belgian visitors. But our chairs were always turned towards the sea.

On some nights, we saw small fishing boats, their powerful lanterns besieged by darkness, cautious and devoted, floating on the back of the water, pilfering fish from the sleeping giant. One night, we saw a largish ship go by, slow and blazing with lights.

"A yacht!" cried Merche.

While it was passing, I was reminded of a funeral of rubbish sailing along the coast, a floating brothel ablaze with yellow lights. It moved presumptuously and solemnly with small, foolish or perhaps drunken steps.

We talked to each other about the sea then and later, when the summer was over, and with other people too. "What's the sea like today?", "We've been to the sea", "We swam in the sea", "The sea was calm", "Which sea was it?", "The Mediterranean", "The water was lovely", "The water was cold at first", "The waves were huge".

And so we continued, then and now, without really understanding or saying anything.

Perhaps it would be easier to talk about the beach. Just that: the beach.

I always felt ashamed and reluctant when I went swimming, although I concealed my feelings from Merche. Because I could sense something beyond the sea. I could sense a secret that was as clear as the water itself, a secret it would never reveal, however long I lived, and which perhaps my mind couldn't even penetrate.

And on a couple of occasions during our stay, without anyone noticing, I would sit with my back to the sea to calm my anxiety, but I didn't do so again, just in case Merche should say to me:

"What are you doing there with your back to the sea? Don't you want to watch me swimming?"

Because she would think that she was on the beach. Whereas, in fact, the beach was in the sea.

NELSON STREET.
CUL-DE-SAC

H E WENT IN, slightly dragging his feet. He was
wearing glasses. His tight, hard lips stretched to
form a smile. His eyes pushed his eyebrows upwards as
if scorning his glasses or trying to jump over them. He
looked behind him and to the right and left, making sure,
it seemed, that no one was there. He paused, then went
over to a corner table by the window. He sat down and
looked out at the street. He turned, raised his head, then
picked up the menu and read it with some indifference.
He put it down on the table and fiddled clumsily with
the knot of his tie; then, with the palm of his hand on his
chest, he nervously smoothed both tie and waistcoat. He
looked over at the door to the kitchen, meanwhile feeling
in his jacket pockets. From the right pocket he pulled out
a newspaper. He placed it on the table. He looked out at
the street. He looked at the folded newspaper. He looked
at the door to the kitchen. He looked up. He sat there,
head raised, broad, flaccid, hairy hands resting on the

table. His lips were moving slightly when the swing door into the kitchen creaked softly open. He turned slowly, abstemiously towards the door. The rheumaticky, varicose waitress, with broken purple veins on her cheeks, rowed over to the table on her fat legs, her weary face making a feeble attempt at friendliness.

"Good afternoon, sir. What can I get you?"

"Good afternoon. Um…"

He hesitated. He trained his eyes, glasses and awkward smile on the menu. He paused as if to indicate that he was drawn to one of the dishes, and the waitress clicked her tongue either so as not to be forgotten or to fill the silence.

"I'll have the steak in breadcrumbs with chips."

"I'm sorry, sir, but there's none left."

"I see. Um…"

He looked at the menu again, this time holding it farther away from him, as if bothered by a reflection.

"I'll have the stewed mince and potatoes."

"There's none left, sir. I'm sorry."

He stretched his mouth still farther until the corners disappeared into two deep crevices. He turned to face the waitress, picked up the menu and held it vertically in front of his eyes, creating a small screen between them.

"Right, right. And the fish? The hake with chips?"

"I'm sorry, sir, that's off too."

He put the menu down on the table and observed the waitress with quiet bemusement, just as the Queen might regard a pink fly that had landed on her, an innocent fly from the Commonwealth.

"I'm sorry, sir, I really am."

"Could you recommend something?"

"Of course. Wait just a moment, please."

"I'll wait."

"Thank you."

He watched her turn, head towards the kitchen and disappear through the door, along with her reluctant, misshapen legs, with their grim clusters of veins, and her elephantine behind, wayward and compact.

The waitress returned and, aware that she was being watched, tried to hurry and attempted a few meaningless burblings, but part of her body lagged behind.

"Would you like some spaghetti?"

"Perfect," he replied rather too enthusiastically, as if that is what he had been intending to eat ever since he arrived.

"You'll enjoy it. It's really delicious!"

He nodded brusquely, and his chin stopped halfway, rather as a flamingo pauses, head down, before spearing some bothersome parasite on its wing.

She withdrew, and he again heard the nasal creak of the swing door; he opened the newspaper, then closed it again and put it down on the table. He looked over at the

kitchen. He looked out of the window. He read the sign
on the corner of the street: "Nelson Street. Cul-de-sac".
Nelson Street led into the avenue where the restaurant
had its entrance; it was made up of detached houses
with one or two garages, long back gardens and various
run-down tenement buildings. The cars driving down
the one-way street passed with youthful impetuosity,
sending out pulses of sound.

On the corner of Nelson Street a middle-aged man
appeared with bristling hair, baggy, drooping trousers,
large eyes and a wrinkled face. He turned on his feet
like an automaton in order to place himself on the edge
of the pavement. Suddenly, standing very erect and
keeping his elbows close to his body, he began to conduct
an imaginary orchestra of percussion and wind instru-
ments. He appeared to be urging the percussionist to
keep banging the cymbals.

The man in the restaurant looked across at the kitchen
door, his now bright eyes adding to his stiff smile; then,
with renewed interest, he immediately turned back to
the man in the street.

The man had crossed the road and was walking calmly
along the opposite pavement towards, it seems, a newspaper kiosk. He disappeared behind the kiosk.

He soon reappeared, striding rapidly in the other
direction, with a folded newspaper under each arm
and another vast newspaper open in his hands. When

he reached Nelson Street, he stepped off the kerb with extreme care, slowed his pace and stopped in the middle of the street, reading intently. "What if a car comes along…", "A car might come along and…", "A car could come round that corner at any moment…" The man rapidly folded up the newspaper he was reading, added it to the other one he was carrying under his left arm and walked over to the opposite pavement taking two hops each on either leg. When he reached the kerb, he climbed onto the pavement by raising his right leg ridiculously high, then set off again, but instead of coming down Nelson Street, he continued along the avenue. Ahead of him, going in the same direction, were two ladies wearing hats and walking along arm in arm. He tiptoed up to them and, keeping one step behind them, began to imitate their swaying, rhythmic walk, like barges bobbing about on the water…

It was difficult for the man in the restaurant to see now, and so he slightly shifted the table, with its bottle of tomato sauce, plates and cutlery, so that he could lean right over and peer out of the other side of the window, his forehead resting on the glass. One of the ladies turned round, spotted the man following them and stopped abruptly. The man immediately averted his gaze, stared haughtily down at the pavement and brusquely, awkwardly—perhaps fearfully, too—marched straight past them, feigning a complete lack of interest. He was walking along very briskly now, when...

The man heard beside him a sound like someone sniffing. He turned his head and looked over his shoulder. The waitress was there with a plate in her hand. He straightened up and sat down, while she pushed the table against the window, restored the sauce bottle and the cutlery to their proper places and set before him the plate of spaghetti.

"Seen something interesting?" she asked.

"Yes, very. Very interesting indeed! Thank you."

The waitress lumbered off, and he began greedily coiling the spaghetti round his fork, using the spoon as bowl. He glanced over at the door to the kitchen and saw that it was not quite closed and that the waitress was peering at him through the crack.

CLOTI

"OK, SEND HER OVER."

And Señorita Palmira, who had three small children and another on the way, put the phone down and said to Toño, who was falling asleep in his armchair:

"She'll never be as good as Rosa."

And she sat down, wondering how things would turn out for Rosa, who had worked for her as a nursemaid for four years and, instead of becoming a nun, as she had always told everyone was her intention, had married a man from the same village as her and with whom she had been in regular correspondence.

"She's going to have a very different life in the village from the one she's had here with us in town," she said, as Toño uttered his first loud snore.

And two days later, the new nursemaid arrived, Cloti, who had the dark pallor of the poor, and was skinny and slightly hunched, having carried children in her arms long before she was really strong enough to do so, and who wore women's clothes that hung loosely about her thirteen-year-old body. She came from the mountains—whether from the Sierra de Saceruela or the Sierra de Almadén, Señorita Palmira couldn't remember—and she had two sisters who were also in service, one with a family in Córdoba and another in Almagro, and a brother who had found a position as a cook or a kitchen hand at the spa at Fuensanta.

"I understand there are five of you, four sisters and a brother."

"Yes, my other sister, Micaela, is in Linares…"

Señorita Palmira stepped back a little.

"Don't shout, girl. And what does she do?"

"We don't know."

"Please, don't shout, I've told you already. I'm not deaf, you know. People in town don't talk the way you folk up in the mountains do."

Señorita Palmira's words buzzed like motherly, loving bees about her mouth, while Cloti seemed to have clambered up onto some high crag, from which she heaped loathing on the earth and sky like a rook.

"That isn't speaking, that's shouting. You see, Cloti, there's always someone sleeping in this house. There's María de las Mercedes, who's not yet one year old; Almudena and Toñito who, like all small children need their sleep and so tend to get up late; then there's my husband, who always takes a nap in his armchair before going back to work; and my father-in-law, who has a lie-down as soon as he returns from his daily game of cards at the local bar; and even the neighbours may take a nap, too, for all I know; you never hear anyone shouting in the courtyard. Imagine if someone were to ask you something about us, however trivial, well, everyone would hear what you said in reply…"

Señorita Palmira spoke in gentle waves and smelt of warm flesh and breast milk.

Cloti got into the habit of clapping her hand over her mouth whenever her loud croak soared up to the heavens, which was all the time, but she simply could not understand this household, because in the big houses in the mountains where she had been brought up, the children and the elderly who slept during the day, regardless of whether they were sleeping in a bed, in a cradle or on the floor, always seemed dead to the world and oblivious to the fact that everyone around them was shouting at the top of their voice and, besides, people there tended to sleep at night and, summer or winter, got up at six or seven o'clock in the morning, if not earlier. It seemed to her that in the city everyone slept very lightly, and the only explanation she could come up with was the one people at home gave for everything: they obviously didn't work hard enough, because a good night's sleep had to be earned, like your daily bread or the trust of your master.

"Cloti, please, Señor Toño is sleeping."

"For Heaven's sake, Cloti, the little one's fast asleep."

"Cloti, cover your mouth, please."

So-and-so's sleeping, someone else is just falling asleep, you've woken him up, or you will wake him up, why do you have to shout so, you'll get the children into bad habits, is that how they taught you to speak at school, what a way to educate children, like savages, when I have the baby, God and St Raymond permitting, you'll either have to change your ways or I'll have to let you go…

Cloti was very confused and couldn't understand why they found her way of speaking so irritating and why, on the other hand, they didn't get annoyed with the television or the ambulances, when the latter sounded as if the patient they were carrying was yelling at the top of his voice, and she began to think that perhaps she lacked some refinement or native cunning common to those city folk, and so she tried to make it clear that she was aware of this by interrupting a sentence with her hand over her mouth in order to speak more softly, giggling and shrugging and repeating her favourite excuse: "That's how I always speak."

Her fatal taste for free speech and for rending the air with her cawing became a source of fear and horror one afternoon when Señorita Palmira sent her to the Church of the Holy Orders with a message for Father Román, the parish priest. Father Román wasn't to be found at home or in the sacristy, so Cloti went to see if he was at church, where she found him praying. Sitting with him in the gloom were a few women whispering prayers, and Cloti went over to the priest's pew and stood there, saying nothing. Father Ramón looked at her, opened a book and sat reading for a good while before, with some difficulty, getting to his feet; then he drew very close to her as if he couldn't quite see her and, in a soft, mellow voice, asked:

"What do you want, child? What do you want?"

"Señorita Palmira sent me to tell you that…"

The priest shrank back, raised his right hand, placed one silencing finger to his lips to stop her, and let out a very long "shhhhh", like a balloon deflating or like an owl in the bell tower.

Cloti had covered her mouth, convinced she had committed some terrible sin. Then she removed her hand from her mouth and said as quietly as she could:

"I'll come back when God is awake."

Then she fled on tiptoe and didn't look back.

MISTAKEN IDENTITIES

Lorenzo is such a worrier! He worries intensely about nothing at all; he's in a constant state about the silliest of things! He began to suspect that the questions people were always asking him and to which he always had to answer No, and the number of occasions on which people mistook him for someone else must all have some basis in reality, in some mysterious truth; perhaps those people were right in a way.

If, for example, a gentleman came over to him and said: "Excuse me, is your name Francisco?", Lorenzo would frown and say anxiously: "No, no, of course not. My name's Lorenzo."

And it wasn't that he thought that this complete stranger Francisco might be a bad person or some rogue wanted by the police. No, Francisco could be anyone. What worried him, what he found so mysterious, was that he could just as easily have been called Francisco as Lorenzo, that he had a certain percentage of Francisco in him, in his gestures, his face, his eyes, his clothes.

He had been worrying about this for almost two years. It began when he was doing his national service and had time on his hands. He was pondering the lives of his commanding officers and thinking how every village has a different way of expressing the same thing. He was teetering on the verge of dialectology. But one Sunday afternoon he was caught unawares by a question. Up until then, he hadn't even really noticed that he was often mistaken for someone else.

"Young man, are you in the cavalry?"

"No, no, I'm not."

"I see. Because in the cavalry, of course, they give you instruction in hand-to-hand combat, swords and other weapons."

The person who asked him this question was an old man. But what of it? In the first place, the gentleman should have been able to see that he was in the infantry. In the second place, what did he mean by all that stuff about "instruction" in various matters? "Wow! Even dressed the way I am, I could still pass for a cavalryman!"

He began to compare himself with the men in the fourth squadron. He studied their coarse, blackened features, their stocky, thickset bodies, their baggy breeches, their nasal voices and their awful jokes. He concluded that he really could have belonged to the cavalry.

He thought: "We are never what we should be. We are impregnated with things that are not ours and never have been." Couldn't the questions people asked him be directed at anyone? Was there anyone so completely himself that he could not be mistaken for someone else? Was he the only one who could be both Francisco and Lorenzo, a cavalryman and an infantryman, an engineer and a bookkeeper for a rather dodgy loan company? One day, you see, he was travelling on the train to Villalba to see his cousin Isabel who had just had an operation. He got off the train. Other passengers got off too. On the platform stood a group of workmen wearing scarves covering their mouths and, as soon as they saw him, they talked briefly among themselves, then two of them came over to him and asked:

"Are you the engineer?"

"The engineer? What engineer? No, no, of course I'm not."

"Oh, sorry. So he's not on this train either. We're waiting for the mines engineer, you see."

They were from Hoyo de Manzanares. They must have been guards or miners. They were waiting for the train so as to receive their weekly wages perhaps or in the hope of finding work. They were waiting for an engineer. Apart from that brief exchange of remarks, they had approached Lorenzo as soon as they saw him. How odd. Out of all the other passengers who had arrived, those men had identified Lorenzo as the engineer. His cousin Isabel found the mistake most amusing. She smiled as if there were nothing else to do in the world but smile, because she was pleased that her cousin had come to see her and because she was ill.

Mistaken identities! What mysterious veil covers the eyes of the person who makes the mistake? What are they trying to tell us with that mistake? What path are they opening up for us? What mysterious essence in us encourages those erroneous questions?

People had been mistaking Lorenzo for someone else long before he even noticed.

"Do you own a hotel in Los Negrales?"

"You'll have had your lunch, I suppose."

"Hi, are you the jeweller from the shop on the corner?"

"Are you related to Señor Requena?"

"Heavens, is that you, Andresito!"

"You probably know Julia already."

"Is your father called Antonio?"

"Did you do your degree in History or in Politics?"

"You look to me like you're from Extremadura."

Good grief! What a world of possibilities people offered him! He was capable of being called Lorenzo, of having his own life and relationships and, at the same time, filling other worlds, too, indeed overflowing them, and having a father called Antonio, being related to Requena, having a university degree, meeting and even marrying Julia and being a native of Extremadura like Hernán Cortés…

But he was just plain Lorenzo. The son of Pedro and Aurora. Born in León. Inhabitant of Madrid. A bookkeeper in Calle de Carretas. Resident in an obscure boarding house in Corredera Baja. He was Lorenzo. The kind of man who comes over all romantic when he sees a clean shirt folded neatly on a wardrobe shelf.

He was Lorenzo, who, on that particular morning, could not decide whether or not to buy a ticket for the football match and was strolling indecisively to and fro in the midday sun in Plaza de Canalejas. Some other men were hanging about, too. And walking slowly along next to him was a pale, very pretty young woman, her hands in her overcoat pockets and her spine slightly arched; she was wrapped up warmly, with a kind of feline grace, looking cold and delicate despite the sun. Lorenzo, strolling idly back and forth between two streets, glanced at her for a moment, then continued his pacing. Suddenly, at his back, he heard an indecipherable hubbub, a slight commotion, and noticed people hurrying to a spot immediately behind him. He turned. The young woman, looking even paler, almost waxen, was lying on the ground in a pose of deathly abandon, as if—or so it seemed—she had been laid low by the thunderbolt of being stood up. He stepped into the circle of six or seven people.

"Are you the boyfriend?" asked an older fellow with moustaches, who revealed himself to be a man of action and took charge of the situation.

"No...no..."

"You're probably still in shock. Come on, help me! If she's just fainted, that's no problem, but if it's her heart, which it might be... Take that arm. That's it. You over there. Come on. Easy does it. Right, now what we want is a taxi. There's one! She needs to be taken to the nearest first-aid post. Come on, man, in you get and don't worry. Come on, lad!"

He felt someone giving him encouraging, affectionate pats on the back. Then someone else grabbed his arms and propelled him into the taxi. When the taxi moved off, the crowd of onlookers on the pavement discussing the incident suddenly increased in number.

He was alone in a taxi with a woman he didn't even know. The taxi driver turned and asked drily:

"So what happened, then? Did she faint? Are you the boyfriend?"

He spoke slowly, with great aplomb, sarcastically savouring every word, as if he were accompanying his questions with a slow handclap. Lorenzo was troubled. People just wouldn't listen. "Are you the boyfriend? Are you the boyfriend?" they kept asking. The boyfriend of this young woman! He stared at her. She had fine features, long, white, manicured hands. She might be in love or she might just be hungry. Her handbag was simple and in good taste, her overcoat thick, warm, elegant...

He had often thought about how other people's mistakes offered him a new life. He had more chances than most of acquiring an alternative identity, of being mistaken for someone else. He could be any one of those mistakes. He demonstrated this by confirming both the question asked by that older man with the moustache and by that impertinent taxi driver: "Are you the boyfriend?"

Yes, he was Laura's boyfriend, Laura being the young woman who had suffered that fainting fit, as transient and spectacular as rain in May. No one was in the least surprised when they got engaged, but he thought privately that some mistakes are like prophecies, mysterious and very troubling...

THE BOOKSTALL

THE STREETS OF THE CITY are like airways, wide-open doors that seek out our vitamin deficiencies and render us prone to catching colds. The streets of the city are good for nothing but wearing away the soles of our shoes, freezing our noses off, finding us a seamstress girlfriend to whom we can boast that our village has a telegraph office and provoking endless, tear-filled yawns and a kind of aggressive sadness that turns our teeth the colour of the winter sun. The boarding house filled Guillermo with a kind of neurotic wisdom. Guillermo was slowly going crazy and, if he hadn't been a strong, serious-minded young man, many would have said that he was already stark staring mad. He played the harmonica and had a good ear for music. He made ox carts out of toothpicks and corks and gave them to Marianín, the landlady's little boy. Every day, after lunch, Marianín would say:

"Go on, make me an ox cart, go on!"

And if Guillermo refused, Marianín would punch him with his hard, strong little fist. Guillermo didn't always make him a cart. Sometimes it just wasn't the right moment to do so, to recall those distant roads. Sometimes it was the moment to chew on a bit of wood, to bat at the light bulb with your hand or to fall asleep. Time was cyclical and various in the streets and rectilinear and monotonous in his room. Guillermo was under the illusion that he wasn't using up time at all. He felt that he was being prepared for death in some other establishment, that he was heading for death in a different ox cart. Time didn't touch or trouble him. He was hoping to beat time and gain eternity through sheer indifference or perhaps through sympathy. When June came around, he would read a few books and pass a few exams. Then, teeth gritted, he would wait to get the results before setting off by train for his village, where he would tramp the fields, drink the local wine and be happy. He had pale eyes, into which the world slipped very easily. He suffered from melancholia, the same kind of enduring melancholia as that suffered by the cricket or the old duck on the pond. He lacked only one thing in order to be happy, which is all anyone lacks. But Guillermo had the advantage that his one thing was very simple.

He found it one rainy afternoon at Juacho's bookstall, as he was walking down the same street he walked down every day. The stall was propped against a convent wall and sold dog-eared old novels and sad magazines. It was made of four planks of wood and two battered crates

covered by a small, dark piece of filthy canvas. The stall
stank, was home to hundreds of small, wingless insects
and resembled a boat wrecked on a cliff—the remains of
Juacho's shipwreck, because Juacho, that seller of detective novels, was a shipwreck victim, the shipwreck having
occurred when he was thrown out of his house, but that's
another story. Juacho had the black bushy moustache of
a stage villain or one of life's tyrants. Leaning on his stall,
he resembled a swarthy, hairy whore, a whore from the
south. He had the body of a navvy, and his laughter was
loud, wry and brazen. He laughed like a young picador.
He had a harsh voice that gave off visible waves and filled
the whole street, a voice that emerged from among the
accumulated dust of all the imaginary police stations
that appeared in those novels and from the occasional
real police station too. However, he never talked about
Scotland Yard, Sherlock Holmes, Maigret, Dog Savage,
the Coyote, the FBI or about the suicidal Max Linder,
the old star of stage and screen. When he spoke, what
he said was pure Madrid.

On the afternoon that Guillermo found the thing he
needed in order to be happy, water was streaming from
the canvas roof onto Juacho's stall. It was raining hard.
The loutish owner of the stall was sheltering in a garage
on the pavement opposite, rubbing his hands together
and calling out to the maids who came running past. The
drenched books were reduced to a paste; the men of the

Wild West were turning the same colour as their hats; on the covers of old magazines, the ink had run onto the white teeth, costly furs and swan necks of the famous stars. And there was Juacho, standing on the pavement opposite, as happy as a sandboy. The stream of water sounded just like water filling a bottle. Something was certainly being filled there; yes, something was gradually filling up.

The following day, in the sun, Guillermo went to look at the books. As they dried, they gave off a lovely, peaceful, bluish steam. Among the steam stood Juacho, like a bookselling saint. The books and their plots were easing back to life with elastic, feminine grace, making delicate crackling noises. Guillermo picked one up and became quite mad with joy. He had to dig in his nails in order to unstick it from the planks. It had become moss like the moss that carpets woods, moss you could buy for a peseta.

Every day at the boarding house, Guillermo would give that wise old novel a squeeze. He would press his nose to the pages in order to smell the earth and the air, the rain and the sun. Were there books anywhere in the world that contained the same deep wisdom as Juacho's books? Was there anything purer and more ancient in the whole city? Those books contained the tunes he played on the harmonica, the ox carts, human time, the joy of walking the earth. Guillermo bought more and more of those battered old novels. He never read them. In one he was surprised and delighted to find a toad. It was a small, dead toad, but it seemed to him very beautiful. Guillermo lived in hope that one day a novel would simply crumble to dust in his hands.

THE ARMCHAIR

ONE MORNING, my mother went shopping and returned in a van belonging to a cabinetmaker, who carried an armchair up to our apartment. When my father got back from work and saw the chair by the window in the living room, he asked:

"Whose is that?"

My mother said:

"I just bought it."

My father looked at her in disbelief and exclaimed:

"You're mad!"

That's how my father always began the story of the armchair, and he told it to me I don't know how many times, because I was only five when my mother bought it, and, besides, he told it to me so that I would take his side.

My mother had been saying for ages that they should smarten the place up just in case Doña Micaela should ever come and see us.

"Doña Micaela is what she is and we're what we are; she has money and we don't…"

"We can pay for it in instalments…"

And so it was that, one morning, she stopped by the cabinetmaker's next to the market, saw the armchair in the window and immediately felt that it would be a good way to start improving the apartment.

This is what the cabinetmaker told her:

The armchair was made of mahogany in the Isabelline style, albeit late Isabelline, because it had springs in the back and the seat. It had belonged to the big house in Calle de Ministriles and had been brought in to be reupholstered, but, unable to find any Nanking silk, he had used artificial Chardonnet silk instead, and, in the end, the Marchioness had told him to keep it, because they had decided to refurnish the whole room…

My mother's eyes were like saucers, and in a tiny thread of a voice she said:

"Unfortunately, I can't afford to buy it…"

"There's no hurry. Pay me in instalments," said the man.

My mother agreed to pay in six monthly instalments, and the cabinetmaker loaded the chair onto his van and drove my mother and the chair home.

All our other furniture was old and second-hand, and if it didn't wobble, it creaked; everything either had a mediocre look about it or appeared to have been born malformed. When my parents got married, they just bought the few bits and pieces they needed and moved straight into the apartment, which was cheap to rent and not so much antique as old. My mother went all out in her efforts to improve our furnishings.

My father never accepted the armchair, not even in the expectation that Doña Micaela might visit us, and, over the years, albeit less frequently as time passed, he would come up with arguments against it:

"That armchair's not for people like us. I'm not going to sit on it."

"A man's posterior doesn't need all that padding."

"The only true revolutionary is the man who sits on the floor."

"Think of all the ham we could have eaten with the money you spent on that chair!"

And if he happened to be in a good mood, he would refer to it as "the sibyl's chair".

"There's no reason why the poor shouldn't have fine things in their homes, too. A fine piece of furniture never looks out of place," argued my mother.

Because of the animosity that had grown up around the armchair and our strained finances, my mother abandoned the idea of improving the apartment, but, whenever she went to pay her monthly instalment, she returned more convinced than ever that it had been a good buy, because the cabinetmaker always told her stories about the chair.

"I wouldn't be surprised if Pepe Botella hadn't sat on that chair."

"Pepe who?"

"King José I, Napoleon's brother, the one who liked his drink. And I'm sure Isabel II would have sat on it, because she often stayed with aristocratic friends, and so did her husband, and General Espartero. I'm not just saying this, I know it for a fact."

"Do you mean the man on the statue, the one riding a horse?"

"The very same."

I sided with my mother, and once, when we went to the Retiro Park, she pointed out Espartero's statue to me as we were leaving and said: "Your father may not believe it, but that very important general once sat on our armchair."

I stood stock still, unable to take my eyes off him, as if I had always known him and he were a close relative of ours.

One day, my father returned from work in a bad mood and it occurred to him to say that he wasn't sure whether to sell that reactionary chair or to adopt a cat so that it would piss on the seat the Queen had sat on and sharpen its claws on the mahogany legs like a true gentleman; without a word, my mother flounced off into the bedroom to cry, and I didn't move a muscle, because my father knew very well that I wanted to go and console her and he didn't take his eyes off me.

When I was alone with my mother, she would let

me play at being king, and if Vidal and Goyo were there—two friends of mine living in the same block—I would sit in the armchair and issue orders, for example, to go to the kitchen and bring me a glass of water and a spoon—because I thought kings drank water as if it were soup—to crawl about the room a few times or to come and ask my formal permission to go forth and discover a new land full of fierce Indians. If they rose up against me, I had to win, although we made sure to engage in any battles well away from the "throne" so as not to damage it, because my mother was always telling me to be careful, and that kings, unlike me, weren't always kicking and fidgeting when they sat on the throne.

I knew Doña Micaela from a photo in which she was holding me in her arms when I was still a baby, and to my surprise and to my mother's delight—because we were alone at home at the time—she finally made an appearance early one afternoon.

As soon as she came in, she cast a rather inquisitive eye about the apartment and immediately noticed the armchair:

"Goodness, have you won the lottery or did you steal it?"

And to play down what she had said, she burst out laughing. My mother lied to her:

"I must have told you the story a hundred times! Don't you remember? It belonged to my great grandmother, who was given it by a very grand lady in the village whose house she'd worked in for many years. Then my grandmother Bonifacia inherited it and, when she died, it came to my mother."

"How amazing, because it looks like new."

"Well, I have had it reupholstered."

Doña Micaela sat down on the chair, and my mother made her coffee and gave her a serviette and a plate and two cakes.

Doña Micaela stroked my hair and said how much I'd grown.

They talked for a long time about people I didn't know, and my father, fortunately, arrived home late, as if he had sensed her presence, and said how pleased he was not to have been there.

"Well, now that she's sat on that piece of junk, we can sell it," he said.

When I heard this, a lump came into my throat and, as soon as I had the opportunity, I asked my mother tearfully:

"Are you really going to sell it?"

"Do you want us to?"

"No."

"Well, neither do I."

And she kissed me.

Now I realize that the "piece of junk" had allowed me to dream of being General Espartero or of being king and having armies at my command. Sitting on it was like passing through the door of hopes and treasures, seeing princesses, living in a palace, oblivious to the smell of sardines or fried peppers. Thanks to my mother, the chair was our one adventure, my one toy, which, even though we were poor, meant that we weren't poor at all and instilled in me a secret dignity that I still, inexplicably, carry within me.

In the end, they did have to sell it, but, by then, I had stopped playing at being king.

OLD MAN DRIVE

T HE DOORBELL only rings when there's a new moon, as if the person calling wanted to melt away into the shadows. Not that I'm expecting anyone at three or four o'clock in the morning, because no one rings the doorbell at that hour. At that hour, I'm either sleeping or grappling with the pillows in an attempt to reconcile them with the elusive sleep I seek, or else, when the dawn breeze makes the blinds click and bang or lifts the curtain like a soft out-breath, I'm feeling my chest just to make sure I'm still alive. At night, I toss and turn between the sheets, and the slightest click or echo in the house makes me open my eyes, cock my ears and wait helplessly for something to happen. Sometimes I do plumb the somniferous depths and then, occasionally, an intense, loud, urgent ringing pierces the normally cautious silence of the night, penetrating every corner and demanding an immediate response. "Oh, no," I mumble and, still half asleep, get out of bed and, from the balcony, peer down through the slats of the blind at the front door and see no one, only the night, which lays itself before me in all its indifference or its pretended candour and silence. I go back to bed and speculate about that invisible night owl demanding my attention and inexplicably perpetuating my disquiet, who resents my rest, who takes advantage of moonless nights to make his very invisibility more obvious and more frightening; the wakeful visitor who both wants and doesn't want to come in, and whom I cannot describe as a thief or a murderer, because he's neither of those things and because he has no name.

I ponder the gratuitous wickedness of someone who wanders the streets at night or perhaps works at night and returns to his lair or walks down my street either filled with resentment or rolling drunk. Someone who doesn't know me, but who, for no reason, rings my doorbell and perhaps other people's doorbells, too, just to make his crime more heinous. I've considered, too, that maybe the low winter temperatures, capable of making the world's ears buzz, could seal up a door with ice and cause a doorbell to shrink back into the precarious warmth of the house. But why does it always happen when the moon is on the turn, the streets deserted and the dawn at its sharpest and darkest, lit only by the street lamp on a distant corner, penned in by shadows?

The night is a universal truce during which we wait for the new day. The absence of light strikes fear into all of us, animals and men; it's a time to lock the doors, speak softly, turn out the lights so that our house will go unnoticed and blend in with all the others in the dark, silent street; a time to feel the hammer of sleep and tiredness, to withdraw into the cave of the bed and surrender to the mysterious realm of dreams, to wake perhaps in the early hours, screaming and fearful or, for some unfathomable reason, smiling, eyes closed, as if beneficent wings had brushed our lips. A time to revisit forgotten remnants of our life, a time for births and silent machine guns that will deliver to the new day millions of newborns and corpses. A time to be spent in the other world, whatever that is, a world expressed in sighs and apparently inexplicable groans, in chafings and sudden buffeting winds and quiet disembodied voices conspiring outside, where you can barely hear or understand them.

Trying to make it seem as if I were talking about something perfectly ordinary, I've asked various neighbours if they ever hear anything unusual in the small hours, and they always say No and, in turn, ask me why, telling me that the owners of No. 52 have installed an alarm that sometimes goes off for no reason and howls away for hours if they happen to be out for the evening, and perhaps that's what I've heard. I shrug and say, yes, they're probably right: "Perhaps it *is* the neighbours' burglar alarm," I say. But it isn't.

My house has two doors, the street door and the one in the living room that opens onto the garden. The garden is fenced and has its own flimsy, apparently lockable gate.

The only bell is on the front door, but I suspect that the person who rings the bell at night is trying to tempt me downstairs to open the front door while he sneaks in through the living room and grabs me from behind, and so now, when I hear the bell, I listen for a moment, then go to a window at the back of the house and scrutinize the shadows in the garden, where the bushes and the trees flourish placidly in the darkness or sway obediently in the night breeze. No one. No one? I try to penetrate the shadows, where I can make out odd shapes and figures that appear to be moving and signalling to each other, but I hear nothing, absolutely nothing, and so return to my cold bed, looking right and left, watching every uncertain, somnambular step I take.

The doorbell ringing at night is an illness no doctors can cure. I used to wake before I even heard it, but now, whenever the moon is on the turn, or, rather, always, I lie waiting for it, unable to sleep, and spend long, sleepless nights wishing the wretched bell would ring, because I can't get to sleep, and if it does suddenly, raucously irrupt into the silence, like a treacherous knife-thrust, like a baleful laugh, I jump out of my skin, then wait a few minutes before creeping out of bed to ascertain whose finger it is pressing the bell, and, after traipsing back and forth in the house, I flop into bed again like a twisted, abandoned, broken body that someone has discarded there.

On two occasions, I opened the front door and stood, looking defiantly out at the night, until the dawn dew invaded my half-naked body with profound, unstoppable shiverings and shakings. On more than three occasions, I opened the door that gives onto the garden and boldly peered behind the trees and among the bushes; I even fell over in the darkness, staggered, somewhat bruised, to my feet and heard incomprehensible, impossible voices coming from a nearby field where the children play on sunny days.

Tonight, if you can call it night, I finally saw something. It must have been about three or four in the morning, and the bell rang, the bell that both kills me and keeps me alive, and, even in my exhausted state, I still had strength enough to half open the blind at the balcony window and there, at last, I saw it, parked right outside the front door, a very long car, black I think, which then moved off very slowly, almost silently, before, with strange solemnity, turning the corner of my street, and that was all it took: that brief presence of only a few seconds was enough to bring me relief, to leave my body feeling lighter and calmer, and then I found myself back in my bed, quite unafraid now, and sure that this time I would sleep really deeply, far deeper than I ever have before.

LAST RITES

D ON ANSELMO'S WIFE calls him Elmi. Anselmo
sounded to her old-fashioned, like the name of
an ointment, and she often said to him:

"Elmi, it's such a shame they didn't christen you Luis
Anselmo or some such thing. It sounds better, more
modern somehow…"

For decades now, Don Anselmo had thought of his
wife as a small, insignificant thing with chicken thighs
and tightly curled, straight-from-the-hairdresser hair,
and, as with curly endives, he always felt there was a
slight bitterness about her. When he met her, she called
herself Candela, and that's what he called her, too, even
though her name was Candelaria.

Candela thought of Elmi as her own personal bear,
because of his slight paunch, which, on some nights, she
would stroke just to show that she wasn't afraid of him,
although she would have been delighted if Elmi the bear
had surprised her occasionally by taking a good swipe
at her or biting her hand off.

Don Anselmo had been a studious and rather

ingenuous youth, and the many pages of the many books he had read drove him into a paroxysm of communicative enthusiasm, which he immediately transmitted to the young people who studied under him, but never to his wife, whom he referred to privately as blotting paper.

Candela could not see the point or the interest in knowing that their neighbour's greyhound, although born in Madrid, was, in fact, of French origin and went by the Latin name of *Canis gallicus*, or that, without the benefit of many centuries of history, she would never have inherited words—or lexical items, as Elmi called them—which she used almost every day, such as rag, step, drama, alcove or tomato.

Don Anselmo spent hours working in his study, sometimes even forgetting to loosen his tie or take off his waistcoat or jacket. This is what he most enjoyed doing, but, for some days now, he had been bothered by the thought of his approaching birthday, which Candela always insisted on celebrating in the entirely selfish and entirely erroneous belief that it would be fun. He always put up with it, the wasted day, the cake and the candles, the banal comments from the inevitable relatives, the unnecessary presents, the vacant smiles and the glasses of champagne accompanied by a raucous rendering of that 'Happy Birthday to You' nonsense. He knew that happiness, if it existed, was something else and not that fraudulent, bogus, foreign idea of "the birthday party".

He looked around him and saw his papers scattered about on a chair, on his desk, in files, in order and in disorder; his filing cabinets full of documents and letters; his books lined up on the shelves or forming towers of Babel on the floor. He was about to turn sixty-eight, and when he departed this world, Candela would summon one of his former students, the most handsome or the least intelligent, to make sense of everything in that room, or else she would sell his books to an antiquarian or second-hand bookseller and either throw his papers in the bin or sell them by the kilo.

He felt a wave of heat sweep over him, and, for a moment, his bankrupt carcass struggled to catch its breath. "Dyspnoea," he said to himself, adding: "from the Greek δύσπνοια," and he smiled.

He heard the key in the front door. Candela was back from doing the shopping, going to the cinema or to the hairdresser's, visiting a friend or a lover, real or imaginary. It didn't matter. He called to her. Behind his steamed-up glasses, his eyes were shining.

"Sit down," he said.

She sat down and asked:

"Have you been thinking about what you'd like for your birthday?"

"No."

There was a silence, then with a faint smile he said:

"Imagine that I'm dead…"

"What do you mean? Have you gone mad?"

"No. These things happen… or don't… Anyway, try to imagine that I am."

"All right, if you insist. You're dead."

"Now I appear to you and I say…"

"After you're dead? How? Where? Here, in your study? Ugh!"

"Yes, I appear to you and I say: 'Petra, do you love me?'"

"And I wouldn't even answer because that isn't my name and I've no idea who Petra is."

"I know, but answer me anyway. Please. Is that so much to ask?"

"Oh, I see, it's a game!"

"Yes, in a way. Petra, do you love me?"

"Yes, Elmi, I do love you. I love you very much."

Don Anselmo gestured towards his books and papers: "Feed my sheep."

"Good grief! Don't tell me there are sheep in the house now!"

Don Anselmo said again:

"Petra, do you love me?"

"Not again. I've told you already, haven't I? Yes, I love you. What more do you want?"

Don Anselmo reached out one arm, made a gesture taking in the whole room, and said:

"Tend my sheep…"

Candela's lips trembled:

"Will you stop it! Why don't you just come right out with it and call me ignorant, call me uneducated, call me stupid! Go on! Isn't that what you mean?"

With tears in her eyes, she leapt abruptly to her feet and left the room, slamming the door behind her.

Don Anselmo sighed and remained sitting where he was for a long time, thinking, not knowing what to do, as if struggling to find the answer to the final clue in a crossword.

PLAY IT AGAIN, SAM

I GOT OFF THE BUS and walked up the steep hill—the part of the journey I always dread—which leads me to the Cosmo Cinema. The film wasn't due to start for an hour and a half, and so I went into the café that bears the same name and forms part of the same complex. At the bar I ordered a cheese sandwich with some ginger preserve. Oh, and a cup of tea, of course. I sat down at a table opposite the mirrors and felt suddenly surprised to see myself there, but then that always happens.

I wasn't really hungry, but I concentrated on eating my sandwich and sipping my tea and couldn't help but notice two coffins going over to the bar, two particularly long coffins. They were both standing up and one was clearly a woman and the other a man. The female coffin ordered a slice of ham with a tomato and lettuce salad, and the male coffin a tuna sandwich. Then—because they clearly didn't know each other—they sat down at separate tables. I had nearly finished my sandwich when another coffin—short but very wide and possibly female—came in and ordered two bars of Nestlé chocolate and a cappuccino. Perhaps she was on a diet.

It was a Monday and there was almost no one there; in fact, one of the young women serving behind the bar spent most of the time scratching her head and yawning, and so when there were still twenty minutes to go before the film began, I slowly got up, went to the toilet—just in case—then proceeded upstairs to the cinema. The usher, the one I like best, was standing at the door and he said very politely that I would have to wait five minutes because people were still coming out from the first showing, which had begun at one o'clock.

When five minutes had passed, he apologized and waved me in, and I went to my usual seat in the second row. Two rows behind me there were only two coffins, but not the same two I had seen in the café; they were the sort—and there are many—of whom it's very hard to say quite what they are. When I went to take my seat, the seat said "Hello", and I looked around just to make sure no one else had noticed and then sat down as if I had heard nothing.

The music started, and I saw thirteen or fourteen coffins filing in, some in couples and others alone, as well as other cinema-goers—albeit not many—of the unclassifiable variety, who looked rather out of place and about whom I never know quite what to think, as if they were going to attack me. Well, you never can tell. One thing is certain: they were not coffins.

The lights went down and, despite the noise, I managed to sleep through the adverts, until, at last, *Casablanca* started, a film I've seen at least seven times before and which I only see again in order to hear what Ingrid Bergman says to the pianist: "Play it, Sam." Then I feel something very deep and very remote stirring inside me and I think of Luisa, which is odd because Luisa and I never got on particularly well. Nevertheless—although quite why I've no idea—I always think of her and the evening we went dancing at the Pasapoga Music Hall. Anyway, that's the only reason I go to see *Casablanca*, and I'll be back at the Cosmo next week, too, because they're showing *Some Like It Hot*, by that amusing director Billy Wilder, and I only watch that in order to hear the final line, when the rich, slightly effeminate little squirt of a suitor says to Jack Lemmon, "Nobody's perfect!" I don't even know how often I've seen it, certainly more often than *Casablanca*; the first time was with my little niece, Emilia, when she was thirteen and had ambitions to be another Marilyn Monroe, but the poor thing never even managed to become another Bette Davis.

When the lights went up and I left the cinema, the usher helped me down the stairs to the ground floor. Ahead of me, swaying slowly, was the long female coffin, the one I'd seen in the bar. There was no sign of the male coffin. The usher took me almost to the front door and said: "Take care of yourself! See you next week!" It's a real pleasure knowing people like him.

THE BENCH

MY SCHOOL WAS NEARBY, but to get there I had to cross the tramlines, and crossing them twice in a day made for a hazardous journey. At first, this meant holding fast to the frantic hand of my godmother, who would say: "Wait!", "Let's go!", "No, not now!", "Quick, run!" Later, I had to cross it alone, looking anxiously this way and that, first left, then right. On our side of the pavement there was a double bench with a back rest in the middle section, and immediately next to it, on the corner, was the local bar; beyond that were three doorways—the last of which was mine—and opposite we could see the ancient trees of La Moncloa.

My godmother would sometimes disappear among those trees and up the slopes of the Parque del Oeste, hand in hand with an army corporal who had been or was about to go to Africa, and to whom his rank and that posting to Africa lent an aura of bravery and manliness. As well, of course, as the added glamour of being here today and gone tomorrow. I accompanied them on a couple of occasions; once, on a short walk among the trees in the square, and once while they were standing chatting on the corner. I didn't know who he was, whether a distant cousin or a friend of someone she knew, but he had a very slow, wheedling way of saying things, full of implied meanings and obscure expressions, as if he were trying to persuade her to do something, although quite what I didn't know. My godmother, a young widow, was diminutive, but quite broad in the beam.

My school was on the mezzanine floor. In the mornings, there was no light on the stairs and very little in the classrooms. I don't remember if I had a male or female teacher, although she was probably female, because, had I gone straight from being with my overly solicitous godmother to being with a man, I would have been sure to notice the change. The teachers at school rewarded those students who could sit for as long as possible with arms folded and in silence, and I can see myself now looking very disciplined and keen, very alert. However, my eagerness to learn at that school proved ill-placed. My shirtsleeves grew crumpled with all those hours of stultifying inertia.

When I left our apartment in the morning, my godmother would wait on the landing, looking down the stairwell, until I reached the hallway and the street door; then she would run out onto the balcony and watch me until I disappeared around the corner. She stayed at home, where I expected to find her when I came back.

A year earlier, the apartment had been a hive of activity, and I thought, wrongly as it turned out, that this was how all apartments were. No, my mother was dying, and a daily procession of relatives and friends came to visit her and my father; they would give me a kiss or gently pinch or pat my cheek. I didn't understand about death, not even when she died. Then came the great void, the silence, my godmother's cheerfully chaotic approach to running a household, the black pinafore they gave me to play in and my dear father, also in black, who worked nights and went to bed in the early afternoon in the now dark, inaccessible bedroom—without my mother.

One sunny day, when there were lots of people out in the street—for ever after, crowds became associated in my mind with loss—two things happened: I had gone out without a handkerchief and when I came back to our apartment from school, I rang the doorbell again and again, but no one answered. I went back down into the street, and, I suppose, looked around, without crossing the road again, at the trees of La Moncloa and at my immediate surroundings. Seeing no one I knew, I set off towards the bar on the corner, where I went over to the bench and sat down with my back to the trams. And what loomed largest for me was not that I had been left alone, but the terrible thoughtlessness that lay behind my not having a handkerchief—which I'm sure I didn't need that urgently—and my whole being softened and crumpled at the thought of the lack of consideration implied by their going out like that without any warning and leaving a small boy without a handkerchief with which to blow his nose or dry his tears, which seemed to me the very height of neglect and carelessness.

A boy I didn't know sat down beside me and, on that sunny noonday street, with the dizzying crowds of people coming and going, I remember telling him that I was sitting on that bench because there was no one at home and I had nowhere to go, that I didn't even have a handkerchief nor was I likely to have one, because my godmother would be in Africa by now with her boyfriend, a corporal in the army, whom she loved more than she did me, and that my situation was grave in the extreme because I didn't know how long I would have to sit on that bench. I think I may even have asked about *his* parents, and he doubtless gave some foolish reply that I have since forgotten.

I can see that scene now and I don't know why I chose a public bench in order to tell my story to a complete stranger and why, with a kind of brilliant sixth sense, I invested that handkerchief with such importance and concocted a lie that soon ceased to be one, because while my godmother didn't go off to Africa with her corporal, she did, a few months later, go back to her parents' house.

I still don't know why I invented that story, but that, I suppose, is what I've continued to do to this day.

AN EPISODE FROM
NATIONAL HISTORY

I REMEMBER THE THICK LIPS, the hiccoughing laugh and the check scarf of that small, skinny boy with innocent eyes and a man's gruff voice, who, at only eleven, poor thing, was burdened with the name of Plácido Dornaleteche, and with whom, at that tender age, I was doubtless unwittingly bound by the shared oddity of our names. We would leave school, go round the corner of Mártires de Alcalá and up Santa Cruz de Marcenado, but we took a very long time to reach the corner of Conde-Duque because we were talking and laughing so much and, when we did arrive, we would continue to stand there chatting, with neither ears nor time for clocks, until he crossed the road and walked along by the barracks to Leganitos, while I continued straight on and went in the street door of No. 4. We were studying for the first year of our *bachillerato* (a shrill word that set our teeth on edge) with names that were full of bounty and light, like Antonio Machado, Helena Gómez-Moreno and Julia or Carmen Burell, and others that were full of fear and foreboding, like that of the miserly-looking man, unshaven, grizzle-haired and wild-eyed, who was the author of at least one book on mathematics—ours—and who would occasionally spin the class globe and then gleefully, noisily spit on it. Like us, he had been weighed down as a child with a problematic name: Adoración Ruiz Tapiador.

I remember Plácido trying to instil in me the radiant hope of his beliefs or, rather, those of his older brother, whom I never met, but who apparently wore—for reasons I did not entirely understand—a blue shirt with red arrows embroidered on the breast pocket and who sang a song that my friend would perform with appropriately martial gestures, and of which I remember only—although possibly not exactly—the first two lines: "Marching along the white road / comes a strong and gallant lad…" And he would ask if I knew Marx. Who? Carlos Marx. And I would say No, although he obviously didn't know him very well either, because he would say, oh, no matter, but what my brother and his comrades want, you see, is the nationalization of that Marx fellow's doctrine; he was Russian or something, an atheist and a good-for-nothing, but he had some useful ideas about bringing bosses and workers together and uniting them once and for all in fraternity and justice. Plácido was like a small, bright, whitewashed window, full of pots of geraniums, through which I could see Madrid and my mother and grand-mother's village flooded with sunlight and happiness, so much so that my sheer impatience to see this change come about quite overwhelmed me with contentment, because in my mother's village there were always a lot of men standing around in the square, and in Madrid we were constantly seeing the riot police cordoning off fires or baton-charging students.

I was due to take my exams that year, 1935–36, and in late March we moved from No. 4 Santa Cruz de Marcenado to No. 9 Españoleto, and I doubtless gave Plácido Dornaleteche my new address, although I had never been to his house and knew only the name of the street.

On 18 July, the offended parties on both left and right decided to improve Spain by destroying it and plunged into a civil war with horrific massacres per-petrated by both sides, and we would-be high-school graduates living in Madrid were unable to continue our studies until well into 1937. We had to stand in long queues in order to satisfy our hunger with lentils, sweet potatoes and sunflower seeds and make day-long walks to vegetable gardens outside the city and to nearby villages, only to return with a loaf of bread or three lettuces, but we boys took advantage of the barricades in the streets to hurl stones at the war, and each evening the radio bulletin about the war wafted out through the open windows, seeming to spread and thicken the blood-dark twilight.

In 1937, our apartment filled up with evacuees: an elderly lady from my mother's village, a couple—friends of the family—and their three daughters, two of my father's sisters, María and Nazaria, along with their husbands and sons, three of whom were intermittently sent off to fight on the government fronts in Talavera and Brihuega, at the battle of Brunete, and at Casa de Campo in Madrid. There were only three of us, but we managed to squeeze another seventeen people into our apartment.

It must have been one day in January 1938 when I came back from school to be informed by my father's indolent new wife, whose usual indifference was made all the more exasperating by her inexactitudes and hesitations:

"A lady came with her son; she said he was a friend of yours."

"Who?"

"Doleteche or Dorteche or something."

"Do you mean Dornaleteche?"

"Yes, that sounds about right."

"And?"

"Nothing. They just came to ask if we could help them."

"Had something happened?"

"I don't know. She said a son or her husband had been killed, or both, I'm not sure."

"Why didn't you ask?"

"Well, she was speaking really softly, almost crying, and because, at that point, your Aunt María came out into the corridor and told them: 'We don't want any fascists here!'"

"And what did they say?"

"What could they say? They left."

I kept grimly pestering both my aunt and my stepmother all afternoon and learnt that Plácido—who had probably been the one who had persuaded his mother to come and ask his old schoolmate for help and who was normally a real chatterbox—didn't say a word, that neither of them was wearing black and that the mother, whom I had never met, had greying hair and was nothing but skin and bone. My Aunt María, who occasionally fancied herself as another La Pasionaria, claimed she had said what she said because her sons— "Your cousins," she screamed—were risking their lives at the front every day, but that didn't mean—she added illogically—that she wished my friend and his mother ill, because God and the Holy Virgin knew that all she wanted was for the fascists to be defeated and for the war to end.

The war ended a year later, and most of us adolescents, for a longer or shorter period, wore the blue shirt, which no longer meant the same as the blue shirt for which my friend's brother and possibly his father had died. For years, Spain's tattered skin was an altar besieged by many funerals, although beneath the black trousers and the blue shirts and the red berets there seethed fierce passions—fear, ambition, guilt, revenge—passions that you could feel incubating in the icy silence of those endless masses for the dead.

And, when our time came, most of us students did our training for military service in the university militias, and it was in one of those long lines of tents, when a captain was doing the roll call, that I heard the name Plácido Dornaleteche, and, as soon as I could get away, I went to look for him, hoping we would be able to reminisce about those conversations in the street after school, our school being the Instituto Calderón de la Barca, a vast house that had originally belonged to the Jesuits until the republicans cleansed it by fire and changed it into a secular institution.

But he wasn't there. Or, rather, Plácido was there in his tent, sitting on his kit bag, but he barely responded to my words and barely looked at me. And it was then that I felt the enormity of that day—which, at only twelve years old, I could have done nothing to avoid—when he and his mother came to my apartment asking for help. His tent was only thirty or forty metres from mine, and we saw and passed each other several times, but we never again spoke. Years before we were born, our French teacher had written a line of verse, saying that one of the two Spains would freeze our hearts.*

* A famous line by the great poet Antonio Machado, who died shortly after crossing the French border, as he fled Franco's troops, along with his mother and his brother José and family. For a few years prior to the Civil War he taught French at the school mentioned in the story.

THE LAST SHOUT

WHEN GRANDMA ANA came to live with us, she was wearing five skirts, one on top of the other, and in each skirt there was a pocket on the right-hand side, and in each pocket, in this order, from the outside in, she kept a rosary, the keys to her house in Villaboscosa, some loose change, a picture of San Francisco Solano and, in the deepest, most private of those pockets, the letter Grandpa wrote to her when they got engaged.

My mother gradually liberated Grandma from her skirts and placed the contents of their pockets, in the same order, in five small boxes: the rosary in box number one, the keys in box number two, and so on. My grandmother resisted at first, because, according to her, she was being stripped of all the things she always liked to have easily to hand, and, besides, despite the heating, she still felt cold; my mother bought her a handbag, which my grandmother rejected, and then some cotton petticoats and a woollen skirt, and, with that, she seemed finally to settle down.

On Sundays, she would open box number three and give me two ten-*céntimo* pieces or one *real*, which wasn't much use to me, because you couldn't buy anything for that price, but my parents always added a little something. Each night, before sleeping, alone in her bedroom, she said the rosary. The keys to her house in the village may have changed, because the house had been sold, but that was where my mother and my uncle had been born and where she had lived ever since she got married, and she always said that, regardless of whether the house had been sold or not, it was still hers, because she visited it every day in her memory and sometimes even rearranged the furniture. She would kiss San Francisco Solano before going to sleep and thank him for everything, and every Friday she would read my grandfather's letter, because it had been on a Friday in May in 1896 that she'd received it.

She had a completely different way of naming the world to the rest of us. Spring was "the greening" or "the sweetness"; summer was "the great unbearable" or "the redness"; autumn was "fall time" or "the yellowing" and winter "hanky time" or "the greyness". And, for her, the last day of life was "the last shout".

"Nowadays," she would say, "people know when the seasons start by the date on the calendar and often can't tell the difference between the greening and fall time. Before, we used to feel it in our hearts, sense it in the smells and in the air. And who in the village knew when one was beginning and another ending? Possibly Don Emerio, the schoolmaster…"

Sometimes, she felt unwell, and Don Luis the doctor would come and see her. On some days, she would have backache or say she was too stiff with rheumatism to move, and yet she never stayed in bed. And if anyone came to visit or our neighbour Petra popped in for a chat, my grandmother would always give the same answer when asked:

"So how are things, Doña Ana? How are you today?"

"Much as you would expect. Waiting for the last shout."

"Why don't you go to bed? Wouldn't you be more comfortable there than sitting in your armchair all day?"

"No, no, I've never been a lie-abed."

That business about the last shout troubled me, because I could never work out if it was death that caused the shout or if the shout caused death, and from that point on I took great care never to shout, come what may.

I thought that all saints were born without a surname, and one day I asked my grandmother why she only kissed San Francisco Solano and not Santa Teresa, my namesake, or San Pedro, my father's patron saint. And why he had a surname while others didn't.

"There've been so many San Franciscos. I suppose it's so as not to confuse him with all the others."

"And why do you kiss him every night?"

"Because he's the saint who was always saying 'Praise God!', which is what I used to say sometimes. And what better thing to say! I'd never even heard of him until María Antonia, Doña Carmen's cook... you remember Doña Carmen, don't you? The lady who used to give you sweets whenever you came to the village? Well, María Antonia lived for a long time in Argentina and, when she lost her husband, she came back to the village with her son, and she used to praise San Francisco Solano to the skies; she told me he was the most important saint in all of South America and that whenever he saw a bird he'd never seen before or a tall, ancient tree, or a fine, broad, fast-flowing river or a range of vast mountains, or any one of the many marvels they have out there, he would gaze up at the heavens and say: 'Praise God!' And I really liked that..."

"And is that why you kiss him?"

"Yes, and because I asked him for something once and he granted my wish."

"What wish was that?"

"Don't be so nosy... Remember, curiosity killed the cat... All right, I'll tell you. Your Grandpa and me wanted to have children, but when more than two years had passed and there were still no children in sight, I began to lose hope. Then, one day, it occurred to me to ask María Antonia's saint, and it worked, because your uncle Raúl was born."

"You mean it was a miracle."

"Well, I don't know about a miracle, dear, but yes, maybe you're right, because having children is a kind of miracle. The thing is that miracles happen so often, they seem normal to us, the morning comes and then the night, the sun and the moon rise and set, the earth gives us harvest after harvest, and we say, 'I'll do that tomorrow' and tomorrow we're still alive to do it. Yes, dear, you're right: reality *is* a miracle..."

Mama was bustling about in the kitchen and heard what her mother said.

"But, Mother, if reality was a miracle, it wouldn't be reality."

My grandmother looked doubtful for a moment and did not respond. Then, as if talking to herself, she muttered:

"I don't know... and neither do you. No one knows. Time passes and brings with it new ideas... and ideas pass, too..."

Quite oblivious to her great age, I was constantly pestering her with questions, and Mama was always telling me off:

"You'll make her dizzy with all your questioning. Leave her alone!"

But one day, when my parents had gone out and Grandma and I were alone, I asked her one last question, although I didn't know then that it would be the last:

"And what about Grandpa's letter, why do you keep reading it? You must know it by heart."

"Almost. But that's not really the point, dear. I read it because it's so lovely, that's all. At the time he wrote it, he saw in me everything he wanted to see in me... and I was probably never like that at all. I mean, in the letter he compares me to a radiant dawn, to a rose, and says he has built a nest for my voice in his heart! What nonsense! Love turned him into a poet. One day you'll enjoy nonsense like that, too. You'll see. Then we got married and, needless to say, we had our ups and downs... because that's what life is like. But we loved each other..."

One morning, she tried to get out of bed and failed. That was the first time we had ever seen her confined to bed, and she kept apologizing—her breathing laboured, her voice weak.

The doctor arrived and, after he had examined my grandmother, he took Mama out into the corridor and said:

"She's very ill. Unfortunately, there's not much we can do. So..."

"But what's wrong with her?"

"The years... the years kill us, without the aid of any grave illness."

Mama took out her handkerchief and dried her tears.

"Will she suffer much?"

"No. She may not even realize. It's better like that. I'm sorry."

My grandmother remained in the same state for two more days, never complaining, apparently concentrating entirely on her breathing.

My father phoned the office to tell them he wouldn't be coming in, and then they phoned Uncle Raúl, and my mother talked for some time to him and his wife Julia, who both arrived at the house the next day. Papa kept pacing up and down as if he didn't know what to do, and then went down to the kiosk to buy a newspaper. Then he dropped into a café for a coffee and returned at midday, and my mother, who couldn't stand his pacing, said:

"Go to work, will you! If there's any change, I'll call you."

He duly went to work and got back home gone eight o'clock. And that night, from one o'clock on, when we heard Grandma apparently muttering to herself, the three of us went into her room and, abandoning all attempts to sleep, sat with her.

I was so terrified that she would utter the last shout, that I barely shed a tear; I really didn't want to hear it.

My grandmother died three hours later and passed into the next world as easily as if she were passing from one room to the next through an open door.

She didn't shout, and, after she had taken her last breath, the house was quite different. The air, grown stale with our wakeful watchfulness, seemed filled with the solemnity of a requiem, and the slightest noise, the scraping of a chair on the floor, seemed to scratch that silence made up of suppressed sobs; even with the lights lit, darkness reigned, and the smell of wax impregnated a night grown suicidal and shadowless, and yet, at the same time, black and eternal. And I understood then how much a lifeless body has to say to us.

I felt cold, my eyes were itchy and heavy with sleep. I opened the balcony window, leant on the balustrade and took a deep breath. A car sped past with its headlights on. The wounding light of dawn was already sidling onto the rooftops, and then, suddenly, I heard an anguished cry stabbing the air and pressed both hands to my breast in horror. I looked fearfully up at the sky and, in the darkness, I thought I saw a bird flying away... I didn't mention this to anyone, because my parents wouldn't even have paused to wonder if it was true. And I wanted it to be true... I wanted that shout to have come from her. Because my grandmother never lied. Do such strange coincidences exist? Does anyone know?

TRANSLATOR'S ACKNOWLEDGEMENTS

This translation is dedicated to the memory of Medardo Fraile, whom I knew for far too short a time. I would also like to thank his wife Janet and daughter Andrea for their enthusiasm and help in translating the stories, Javier Jiménez-Ugarte, who encouraged me to find a UK publisher for the stories, Annella McDermott for her invaluable advice, and Ben Sherriff, who was, as always, my first reader.

DATES AND PLACES
OF FIRST PUBLICATION

From *Cuentos de algún amor* (1954): 'Mistaken identities'/'Las equivocaciones'; 'Typist or Queen'/'Mecanógrafa o reina'; 'The Bookstall'/'El puesto de libros'; 'What is going on in that head of yours?'/'No sé lo que tú piensas'; 'A Shirt'/'Una camisa'; 'Child's Play'/'Un juego de niñas'

From *A la luz cambian las cosas* (1959): 'Things look different in the light'/'A la luz cambian las cosas'; 'The Cashier'/'La cajera'; 'The Album'/'El álbum'; 'Berta's Presence'/'La presencia de Berta'; 'The Lemon Drop'/'El caramelo de limón';

From *Cuentos de verdad* (1964): 'That Novel'/'Aquella novela'; 'Restless Eyes'/'Ojos inquietos'; 'Reparation'/'El rescate'; 'Full stop'/'Punto final'; 'Nala and Damayanti'/'Nala y Damayanti';

From *Descubridor de nada y otros cuentos* (1970): 'The Car'/'El coche'; 'Señor Otaola, Natural Sciences'/'Señor Otaola, Ciencias'

From *Ejemplario* (1979): 'The Sea'/'El mar'

From *Cuentos completos* (1991): 'Nelson Street, Cul de sac'

From *Contasombras* (1998): 'The Bench/'El banco'; 'Cloti';
'An Episode from National History'/'Episodio nacional'

From *Escritura y verdad: cuentos completos* (2004): 'The Letter'/'La carta'

From *Antes del futuro imperfecto* (2010): 'The
Armchair'/'El sillón'; 'Play it again, Sam'; 'Old
Man Drive'; 'Last Rites'/'Postrimerías'

Previously unpublished and undated: 'The
Last Shout'/'El día del grito'

PUSHKIN PRESS

Pushkin Press was founded in 1997. Having first rediscovered European classics of the twentieth century, Pushkin now publishes novels, essays, memoirs, children's books, and everything from timeless classics to the urgent and contemporary.

This book is part of the Pushkin Collection of paperbacks, designed to be as satisfying as possible to hold and to enjoy. It is typeset in Monotype Baskerville, based on the transitional English serif typeface designed in the mid-eighteenth century by John Baskerville. It was litho-printed on Munken Premium White Paper and notch-bound by the independently owned printer TJ International in Padstow, Cornwall. The cover, with French flaps, was printed on Colorplan Pristine White paper. The paper and cover board are both acid-free and Forest Stewardship Council (FSC) certified.

Pushkin Press publishes the best writing from around the world—great stories, beautifully produced, to be read and read again.